H HARLEQUIN®

ᴷISS™

S0-ARB-722

THE GUY TO BE SEEN WITH

He paused for a moment, just as his lips were millimeters from her. Her pulse lurched and her breath came in uneven bursts.

And then he was kissing her, expertly wiping any protest away with his firm lips. Chloe clung to his shirt for support. The difference in their height meant she felt she was arching back over the railing, feeling as if she'd fall at any moment.

But even that fear was quickly erased by the sensations erupting through her body. Sweet heaven, this was better even than she'd imagined it would be. He knew just when to take, just when to tease...just how to leave her breathless and dizzy, even without the use of his hands, which were still making sure she stayed right where he wanted her.

If Chloe had been able to string a coherent sentence together, she'd have been able to tell him it wasn't necessary. As much as her brain was screaming for her to run, her body had been waiting too long for this. It was going to enjoy it while it lasted.

And enjoy it she did.

DEAR READER,

I'm very excited to be writing for brand-new Harlequin KISS.
If I could have had a "fantasy" Harlequin line, picking and
choosing my favorite authors so I could find them in one place,
KISS would be it. I can hardly wait to read all the books myself,
and I hope you're going to find some firm favorites and new
authors to love, too.

I'd always intended to one day set a story in Kew Gardens in
London. It's a beautiful place, full of Victorian greenhouses,
grottos, temples, stunning borders and lots and *lots* of trees.
But I could never find a hero or heroine that fit the setting,
so I put the idea on the back burner and let it simmer.

Then last year I was asked if I would like to write a Valentine's
Duet with the wonderful Nikki Logan. I immediately said yes,
and Nikki and I began the planning process—not easy when we
live on opposite sides of the globe. However, one morning (for
me) we were video messaging and Nikki noticed something in
the room behind me. "What's that green thing?" she asked.

I had to laugh. My husband has a hobby.... No, *hobby* is not
the right word. My husband has an *obsession* with growing
carnivorous plants, and one of the reasons I know Kew so well
is our frequent trips to visit the insect-eating plant displays
there. Anyway, a couple of years ago I bought him a stuffed toy
that looks a bit like a Venus flytrap from Kew's shop, and that
was what Nikki had seen behind me. It got us talking about a
possible job for a hero.

And that was how Daniel Bradford sprung to life. Finally,
I had a character to go with my setting.

I hope you enjoy Daniel and Chloe's story—I had the most fun
writing it! And don't forget to check out Nikki Logan's book
How to Get Over Your Ex to read Georgia's story, and find
out how one failed Valentine's proposal brought her love and
happiness, too.

Blessings,

Fiona Harper

THE GUY TO
BE SEEN WITH

———

FIONA HARPER

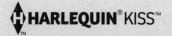

Recycling programs
for this product may
not exist in your area.

ISBN-13: 978-0-373-20706-0

THE GUY TO BE SEEN WITH

Copyright © 2013 by Fiona Harper

www.Harlequin.com

ABOUT FIONA HARPER

————

As a child, Fiona Harper was constantly teased for either having her nose in a book or living in a dream world. Things haven't changed much since then, but at least in writing she's found a use for her runaway imagination. After studying dance at university, Fiona worked as a dancer, teacher and choreographer, before trading in that career for video editing and production. When she became a mother, she cut back on her working hours to spend time with her children, and when her littlest one started preschool she found a few spare moments to rediscover an old but not forgotten love—writing.

Fiona lives in London, but her other favorite places to be are the Highlands of Scotland and the Kent countryside on a summer's afternoon. She loves cooking good food and anything cinnamon-flavored. Of course she still can't keep away from a good book or a good movie—especially romances—but only if she's stocked up with tissues, because she knows she will need them by the end, be it happy or sad. Her favorite things in the world are her wonderful husband, who has learned to decipher her incoherent ramblings, and her two daughters.

This and other titles by this author are available in ebook format—check out Harlequin.com.

If you love this, look out for the first book in the duet, *How to Get Over Your Ex* by Nikki Logan

For Nikki, an all-round inspiration and great gal to work with! And for Andy, my own Indiana Jones with secateurs. x

THE GUY TO
BE SEEN WITH

ONE

___

    Daniel always grumbled that his mobile phone rang at the most inconvenient of moments, and it didn't disappoint him now. Just as he was lifting a delicate Venus flytrap out of its pot, his hands full of roots and compost, his trouser pocket buzzed. Since he refused to assign fancy ringtones to everyone in his contact list the double ring of an old-fashioned phone told him precisely nothing about the caller's identity.

Once upon a time, he'd have ignored it—his hands being full of an uprooted *Dionaea muscipula* and all—but these days he could never quite push the thought from his mind that it might be his younger sister, telling him she was ill again. Or worse, a stranger telling him she'd collapsed and was in Accident and Emergency, and casually requesting he pick her kids up from pre-school.

Reluctantly, he shook the earth off his right hand, cupped the clump of roots and foliage in his left and fumbled in the thigh pocket of his cargo trousers for his phone. He balanced the handset on his shoulder and squeezed his cheek onto it to keep it in place as he attempted to brush more of the compost that caked his fingers off on the back of his trousers.

'Yup.'

The phone started to slide and he quickly grabbed for it with his still-dirty hand.

'Daniel Bradford?' a deep yet annoyingly upbeat male voice asked.

'Yup,' he repeated, more focused on trying to replace the prize specimen in its pot with the use of only one hand. It wasn't going well. He wasn't planning on dividing this one for propagation yet but it was threatening to do just that.

'Well, Daniel, this is Doug Harley and you're live on Radio EROS, London's most romantic radio station!'

Daniel stood up straight, then twisted round, scanning the tropical nursery at London's famous Kew Gardens, expecting to see a group of snickering underlings hiding behind a palm in an adjacent room of the sprawling greenhouse. This had to be a prank, right? And, if there was one advantage of working in a place where ninety per cent of the buildings were made of glass, it was that there was nowhere to hide. He'd find them and make their lives hell for this.

But all he could see was a lone horticultural student, wheeling a trolley of seedlings past the door, plugged into his music and oblivious to the world. The rest of the multi-roomed greenhouse was unusually quiet.

'Daniel?' the silky smooth voice crooned in his ear.

He pulled the phone away from his head and stared at the display, seriously considering just hanging up. He didn't have time for this.

'What do you want?' he barked at the man as he put the phone back up to his ear. 'I'm busy.'

There was an equally smooth—and equally irritating—chuckle on the other end of the line. 'Not too busy for this, Daniel. I promise you.'

He clenched his jaw. The over-familiar manner in which the DJ kept inserting his name into every sentence was getting on his nerves.

'Convince me,' he said.

The chuckle again. As if the man was the insider to some joke that Daniel didn't know about. His eyes narrowed.

'I'm sure you know what day it is today, Daniel?'

Confusion wrinkled his brow further. It was Tuesday. So what?

Oh.

He swore inside his head, remembering the collection of red and pink envelopes that had been sitting on his desk when he'd arrived for work this morning. He'd shaken his head, pushed them to one side unopened and had done his best to forget about them. Not just any Tuesday, but one slap-bang in the middle of February.

'Or what year it is...' the voice added.

Daniel let out a huff. He'd been right all along. A half-baked radio contest run by some sappy station he'd never heard of. He was pretty sure he didn't want whatever prize this idiot was offering. Seriously, couldn't they come up with a better question than what year it was? Even his four-year-old nephew could answer that one. He was just about to tell Mr Silky Smooth that when he was interrupted.

'Of course, leap years have their perks,' the man

said, and a rumble of perfectly pitched deep laughter followed. 'We know it's a couple of weeks until the twenty-ninth, but we've got a Valentine's surprise for you, Daniel. There's a young lady who'd like to ask you something.'

Daniel looked down at the plant in his hand. Even in its current uprooted state, a fly was attracted to the sweet nectar oozing from the glands in its trap. It darted around, weaving in and out of the leaves, looking for somewhere to land.

'Dan?' This voice was soft and feminine. One he recognised instantly.

He froze. His brain told him what was coming, but he refused to believe it.

'*Georgia?*'

That hadn't come out right. He'd sounded grumpy and defensive, not pleasantly surprised, at hearing his girlfriend's voice. He tried again. 'What are you doing?'

Nope. That hadn't been any better.

He heard her swallow in a great gulp of air. 'Daniel...I know you've had a tough time recently, and I've been happy to be there for you...but things are looking up now and I really believe we could be good together.'

Daniel's mouth moved but no words—not even any sounds—came out.

He wanted to close his eyes, as if doing so could block out the sound of her voice, but he was transfixed by the sight of the fly settling on the fleshy pad of one of the plant's open traps. He shook his head, warning the insect off.

Fly away. Escape while you still can.

'So, what I'm doing, Daniel...' She paused, gave a little nervous laugh. 'What I'm saying is...is that I'd like you to marry me.'

In one swift, smooth motion the flytrap closed over the fly. Not so much a snapping as an elegant but relentless squeezing. Daniel could hear the creature's frantic buzzing, see it struggling in the trap as the teeth-like cilia closed tighter and tighter over its head.

Don't. Struggling only makes it worse.

A terrible silence settled around him. All sound disappeared. Even the visitors to the botanical gardens, who could often still be heard from the private nurseries, had hushed. It seemed the whole of London was holding its breath, waiting for his answer.

'Is this a joke, George?' he croaked, a horrible pleading tone in his voice.

This wasn't the Georgia he knew. The nice, uncomplicated, undemanding woman he'd been seeing for almost a year. His Georgia knew he didn't have the emotional space for a proper relationship right now, let alone a marriage. His Georgia understood that and accepted that. So who was this, borrowing her voice and asking him out-of-the-blue questions—on the *radio*, for heaven's sake? Not even person to person, face to face.

Who proposed in public, anyway? It should be done privately and quietly. Preferably to someone other than him.

He squeezed his teeth together to stop himself from demanding an explanation, right here, right now. He was suddenly furious with her for springing this on him, for changing the rules and moving the goalposts of their relationship while he hadn't been looking. This wasn't what they were about and she knew that.

At least, he'd *thought* she'd known that.

Silky Smooth chuckled again. 'Well, Georgia, you seem to have rendered the poor man speechless! What do you say, Daniel? Are you going to put this gorgeous girl out of her misery or what?'

That doused his billowing temper quick smart.

What *was* he going to say?

He could imagine Georgia sitting there at the radio station, a fixed smile on her face and fear in her eyes, bravely trying to pretend it was all right, when really her heart was pounding and her eyes filling.

It wasn't that Georgia wasn't a lovely woman. She was determined and intelligent and sensible. Any man would be lucky to have her. He should *want* to say yes.

But he didn't.

He really didn't.

He wasn't ever going to go down that road again, no matter how lovely the woman in question.

There was a crackle on the line and noise started filtering through again—the hiss of the automatic misting system in the nursery next door, the squeak of a door farther down the corridor, a plane flying low overhead on its way to Heathrow. And Daniel was suddenly very aware that more than a hundred thousand pairs of ears might be listening to this conversation, of just how public and complete his girlfriend's humiliation would be if he gave her the wrong answer.

Unfortunately, where he and Georgia were concerned, the wrong answer was the right answer.

He didn't love her. He wasn't sure he ever would, and she deserved better than that. Gently, he balanced his phone on his shoulder again and carefully put the now-satisfied Venus flytrap plant back down in its pot.

He should have known their relationship wouldn't stay in wonderful, comfortable stasis they'd created. In this world, things moved on, grew, or they decayed.

He'd first met Georgia when Kelly had been halfway through her chemo. She'd been easy to be around. She'd helped him forget that his little sister might not see another Christmas, to forget that his rat of a brother-in-law had run off with his personal trainer and left his shell-shocked wife to deal with a cancer diagnosis—and two under-fives—all on her own. Without Georgia, he'd have hunted Tim down and fed him, bit by bit, to the largest and ugliest *Nepenthes* in his collection.

Daniel shook his head. The Venus flytap was completely closed now; he couldn't even see the squirming fly inside.

He should have known that, eventually, Georgia would get ideas. The awful situation they were in now was as much his fault as it was hers. She wasn't really asking anything horrendous of him, was she? But she was asking for something he wasn't capable of. Not any more. And he'd been very clear about that.

'I'm sorry...' he said, more for not paying attention to what had been growing right under his nose than for what he was about to say. 'We weren't heading for marriage, I thought you knew that...That's what made our thing so perfect...'

Our thing... Subtle, Daniel.

He could hear her breathing on the other end of the line, and he wished he could see her face to face, explain, without listening ears hanging on every syllable.

'It's okay,' she said, and he could hear the artificial brightness in her tone, could almost see the sheen in her eyes. He felt as if he'd been kicked in the chest by a horse.

He shook his head. No, it wasn't okay. He was hurting her horribly, but that didn't mean he could say yes and condemn them to a lie that would ultimately make them both unhappy. He had to do what was best for Georgia, for both of them. He had to set her free for someone who could give her what she wanted.

'I can't, Georgia. You know why I can't say yes.'

There was a moment of ghastly silence and then the DJ began talking again, laughing nervously, trying to smooth things over. Daniel didn't hear any of his words. He didn't even notice when music started to play in his ear.

He felt like a worm.

No, worse than that, because worms were useful, at least, and they didn't harm anything.

He picked up the unearthed flytrap, plastic pot and all, and flung it against the wall of the carnivorous plants nursery. It hit the glass with a resounding bang that echoed over half the gardens. The cracked pot fell away, and the frail plant followed, landing with an almost soundless thump on the floor. Compost that had smeared against the glass began to crumble away and rain down on top of it.

That was when the disadvantages of working in a greenhouse made themselves apparent. Half a dozen curious pairs of eyes stared at him from various parts of the nursery. They must have thought the Head of Tropical Plants had lost his mind.

Or worse. They might have been listening to the radio.

Daniel closed his eyes, ran his hand through his hair, then swore loudly when he realised his fingers had still been covered in peat and perlite.

He opened his lids to find no one had moved. He glared at each and every pair of staring eyes in turn. 'What?' he yelled and, as one mass, the underlings scurried away back into their holes.

All he wanted was for this awful, consumer-fuelled excuse of a day to be over, so he could get back to normal, live his life without anyone listening to what he was saying or spying on what he was doing.

God, he hated Valentine's Day.

Daniel froze as he was crouched down, his hand on the papery flute of a *Sarracenia*. Sunlight streamed through the glass roof, warming his back, and around him visitors milled, casually inspecting the exotic plants of the Princess of Wales Conservatory, one of Kew's modern glasshouses. All in all, it seemed like a normal March day.

Except that, as he worked, the fine hairs on his arms and the back of his neck lifted.

He stood up and glanced around. He was in a vast greenhouse with ten climate-controlled zones, so it would be stupid not to expect people to see him, but it was more than that. It felt as if someone was *watching* him.

Georgia's flopped Valentine's proposal had produced a flurry of unexpected media attention. More than once in the last month he'd found himself staring at the business end of a paparazzo's lens as he was trying to work. But that hadn't been the only unwanted side-effect of publicly humiliating his ex-girlfriend. Now there seemed to be eyes on him everywhere, watching him, judging him.

Until his sister's illness had forced him to come back to England, he'd loved his job working from Kew's base in Madagascar. He'd loved being a seed hunter—searching out rare plants to collect their treasure, tracking down nearly extinct species. But this bizarre media interest made him feel much more like the prey than a hunter, and he didn't like that one bit. No, not a role reversal he was comfortable with.

He finished checking the fine white and green patterned flutes of the pitcher plant and pushed open the door of the small Temperate Carnivorous Plants area and entered the much larger Wet Tropics zone. Here the heat-and-moisture-loving tropical varieties grew, including a large draping display of green and warm purple hanging pitchers. He worked methodically through the twisting tendrils, looking for dried out pitchers that needed to be dead-headed, checking for disease and parasites.

That was when he heard them.

'Do *you* think he looks like Harrison Ford?' a feminine voice said in a not-so-quiet whisper. 'I'm not sure. He's more like that one from the spy series on BBC.'

Daniel froze and imagined a horrible, jungle-related death for the reporter who'd jokingly compared him to the film legend. While the journalist had obviously been quite pleased with his 'Indiana Jones with secateurs' crack, Daniel hadn't heard the end of it from his mates.

'Not sure,' a second voice said thoughtfully, and just as loudly. 'But he's definitely got that brooding, intelligent-but-dangerous thing going on. Have you seen those arm muscles...?'

There was a muffled snort from the first speaker. '*Arms?* I was too busy checking out his nice, tight little—'

Right. That was it.

He was fed up of being treated like a piece of meat, something to be stalked and discussed and ogled. Perhaps he should just jump up on one of the earthy beds and sit there with the plants, because as far as he could see he'd stopped being one of the staff and had morphed into a prime attraction.

When would this end? It was bad enough that the London press had picked up on his and Georgia's story and run with it like a greyhound on amphetamines. They'd been the subject of countless column inches, magazine features and chat show discussions—not that either of them had fuelled it in any way by agreeing to speak or be interviewed. It seemed the whole of the city had been split down the middle, divided into two camps, one supporting him and one supporting her.

But the whole situation had a nasty little side effect, too.

He'd now become The One That Got Away. An irresistible label to the female population of London, it seemed, because en masse they'd decided it was an open season. Every day for the first couple of weeks after the proposal they'd appeared in ones and twos like this, coming to the gardens specifically to track him down.

But it had been quiet for almost a week, and he'd finally hoped it was all petering out. No such luck.

Not that a bit—or even a lot—of female interest bothered him in the slightest. He was as open to it as the next guy. But this was different. They didn't know when to stop. They acted as if they hadn't heard the proposal on the radio, as if they didn't know he wasn't in the market for love, let alone marriage. The whole thing was just stupid. And very irritating.

He was dragged back into the present by a heartfelt sigh behind him. They'd moved closer.

'Shall I go and ask him for his autograph,' one said.

That was it. Hunter or not, Daniel was out of there. He turned and walked briskly down the path, down the steps to the aquatic exhibit half hidden under a manmade 'hill' in the centre of the conservatory, and ducked through a short tunnel to come out on the other side of the zone. He then climbed the path that led him to the upper levels on top of the hill, then doubled back through the ferns and down some more stairs.

He knew this labyrinthine glasshouse like the back of his hand and it wasn't more than a minute before he was crouching down and peering at the two women from a vantage point inside the orchid display. He could have left and gone back to the propagation greenhouses, he supposed, but he liked the idea of turning the tables, of watching *them* hunt fruitlessly for him, before disappearing for good. It would restore his sense of balance, of control.

Now he could see them, his eyes popped. They were over seventy, for goodness' sake! All sensible shoes and nylon trousers. He could see them looking around, having a minor disagreement about which way they should go to pick up his trail.

He almost chuckled to himself. Almost.

At least, he might have done if those hairs on the back of his neck hadn't prickled again.

Seriously? Another one?

He was tempted to turn round and let loose, but he knew he had a bit of a temper, and having a supposedly 'dangerous' edge didn't mean he was allowed to attack paying visitors then use them for lovely, nutritious compost for his favourite plants. There were laws against that kind of thing. Unfortunately.

He was just going to have to bite his tongue and leave. However, if this Valentine's fuelled media circus didn't end soon, he'd be stuck in an office or a greenhouse, not able to go about his job as he pleased, and he'd hate that. It had been hard enough to leave the field and take this post in the first place; he'd only done it because Kelly had needed him to come home and help look after her and the boys.

'Why, if it isn't Indiana himself!' a husky female voice drawled. 'Although I was led to believe you'd swapped the whip for a pair of secateurs these days.'

Daniel swivelled around, still crouching. The first thing he saw was a pair of hot-pink kitten heels with polka dot bows on the front. Definitely not a pensioner, this one. His gaze was inevitably drawn up to a pair of slender ankles and then to shapely calves. For a moment, he forgot all thoughts of running.

Then there was the black pencil skirt. Tight round a pair of generous hips, hugging the thighs... He swallowed.

'So where are they?' she asked.

That was when he realised he was still half squatting. He looked up, past the form-fitting pink blouse to the face on top of it. Red lips. That was what he saw first. Vibrant red lips.

Who'd cut the water supply off from his throat? He swallowed again. 'What?'

Stand up. You're kneeling at her feet, looking like a drooling Neanderthal.

Thankfully, his brain cooperated this time, sending the message to his legs to straighten, and he stood. Finally, he was looking down at her instead of up. Only, it didn't help much. From down below the view of her impressive cleavage hadn't been so obvious. Now his brain was too busy working his eyeballs to do the talking thing.

'The secateurs,' she said with a slight twitch of one expertly plucked brow. 'Are they in your pocket?'

Daniel nodded dumbly and pulled them out. She was blonde. Marilyn Monroe blonde. With shoulder length waves that curled around her face.

'Shame,' the lips said. 'And there was I hoping you were just pleased to see me.'

His mouth hung open a little. Brain still struggling. Much to his disgust, he managed a faint grunt.

'Sorry...couldn't resist,' she said, and offered her slim hand. 'Don't you just love Mae West?'

Daniel stared at the hand for a second or so, at the long red fingernails that matched her lips, then a movement at chest level distracted him. A staff pass on a lanyard was around her neck but, due to the impressive cleavage it was hanging just below, it was twirling gently in some unseen breeze, the photo and name obscured.

She frowned slightly. 'Not a Mae fan, then.'

He nodded, but he wasn't sure if he was agreeing or disagreeing.

'Chloe Michaels,' she said, grabbing his hand and shaking it firmly. 'Orchid specialist and new girl at Kew.'

'Daniel Bradford,' he said, shaking back vigorously. Maybe a little too vigorously. He let go, but then he didn't seem to know what to do with his hand. He stuffed it back in his pocket.

'I know,' she said, and a wry smile curved those red lips.

'You've read the papers...'

She gave a little shrug. 'Well, a girl would have to be dead to not have seen something of your recent press coverage. However, I knew who you were before that. I've got one of your books at home.'

Air emptied from his lungs and he felt his torso relax. Plants and horticulture. Finally, he'd come across a woman who could talk sense. 'Nice to meet you,' he said. And he genuinely meant it.

She just nodded and the smile grew brighter. 'The guys in the tropical nursery said I'd find you here, and I just thought I'd come and introduce myself,' she said, turning to leave.

Daniel had just started to feel somewhere close to normal again, but her exit gave him another view he hadn't quite ready for... The way that pencil skirt tightened round her backside was positively sinful.

She looked over her shoulder before she exited the temperate orchid display through the opposite door.

Daniel snapped his gaze upwards. She hadn't caught him checking her out, had she? That was a schoolboy error.

'By the way,' she said, nodding in his direction, 'incoming at eleven o'clock.'

He hadn't the faintest idea what she meant, but it wasn't until she'd disappeared into the next zone that he even started to try and work it out.

A bang on the glass above him made him jump. He pivoted round and looked up to find his two pursuers in the fern enclosure at the top of the stairs, faces pressed up against the glass, grinning like mad.

Oh, heck.

One of them spotted the door further along the wall. Her eyes lit up and she started waving a pen and a notepad at him.

Daniel did what any sensible man in his position would have done.

He ran.

TWO

———

A skirt this tight and heels this high did not help with an elegant exit, Chloe thought as she kept her back straight and cemented her gaze on the door. She'd thought she'd need the extra confidence her favourite pair of shoes gave her this morning but, when they were teamed with the skirt, every step was barely more than a hobble, and it took a torturously long time until she was out of the orchid display area and amidst the agaves and cacti of the adjoining section.

She paused for a heartbeat as the glass door swung shut behind her, then blinked a few times and carried on walking.

He hadn't recognised her.

She'd been prepared to go in smiling, laugh that embarrassing incident in their past off and put it down to not being able to hold her liquor. In short, she'd planned to be every bit as sophisticated as her wardrobe suggested she could be.

But she hadn't needed to.

She pressed a palm against her sternum. Her heart was fluttering like a hummingbird.

That was good, wasn't it? That he hadn't connected Chloe Michaels the horticultural student with Chloe Michaels, new Head Orchid Keeper. They could just start afresh, behave like mature adults.

Inwardly, Chloe winced as she continued walking along the metal-grilled flooring, past an array of spiky plants from across the globe.

Okay, last time they'd met, Daniel Bradford hadn't had any problems behaving maturely and appropriately. Any *mis*behaving had been purely down to her. Her cheeks flushed at the memory, even all these years later.

She was being stupid. He must have taught loads of courses over the years, met hundreds of awestruck students. Why would he remember one frizzy-haired mouse who'd hidden her ample curves in men's T-shirts and baggy trousers? He wouldn't. It made sense he hadn't even remembered her name.

Or her face.

That, too, made sense. She looked very different now.

This Cinderella hadn't needed a fairy godmother to give her a makeover; she'd done it herself the summer she'd left horticultural college. No pumpkins, no fairy dust. Just the horrified look on Prince Charming's face had been enough to shove her in the right direction. The Mouse was long gone; long live the new Chloe Michaels. And she'd been doing a very good job of reigning supreme for almost a decade.

Only...

A little part of her—a previously undiscovered masochistic part of her—had obviously been hoping he *would* remember, because now disappointment was sucking her insides flat like a deflated balloon. She sighed. She never had had any sense where the gorgeous Daniel Bradford had been concerned. But show her a human being with a double X chromosome who did.

It was something to do with those long legs, that lean physique, those pale green, almost glacial eyes. Add a hint of rawness to the package, the sense that he'd just barely made it back from the last expedition into a dark and remote jungle, and it tended to do strange things to a girl's head.

Maybe that could explain the way she'd acted back there, the things she'd said...

Mae West? What had she been thinking?

While she knew the 'new and improved' Chloe had easy self-assurance, there was confidence and there was sheer recklessness. She'd intended to be calm and professional. She certainly hadn't intended to tease him... *flirt* with him.

However, a little voice in her head had been pushing her, feeding her lines, especially when his eyeballs had all but popped out of his head when he'd been trying to read her spinning name tag. There had been something so satisfying about seeing him that close to drooling that she just hadn't been able to stop herself.

It wouldn't happen again, though. Couldn't.

But Chloe's lips curved as she pushed the main door of the conservatory open and walked out into the spring sunshine. She wiped the smile off her face—literally—with a manicured hand and shook her head.

It didn't matter just how much saliva had pooled in the bottom of Daniel Bradford's mouth when he'd looked at her, because she was never, ever going down that road again. And it didn't matter just how ferocious the monster crush she'd had on him ten years ago had been, because there was one thing she was certain of...

She'd shoot herself before she got within kissing distance of him ever again.

Daniel hung from a spot halfway up the climbing wall at his local sports centre and peered down at the top of his friend's helmet. 'Hurry up, Al,' he called out. 'You're out of shape. Must have spent too much time lolling on a sun lounger while you were on holiday.'

Alan eventually caught up. He wasn't looking as chirpy as normal.

'What's up with you?' he said, still panting. 'You were up this wall like the hounds of hell were on your tail, and you only climb like that when trouble's brewing— usually woman trouble.'

Daniel shrugged and pulled a face. 'Of a sort.'

Alan grinned at him hopefully.

'Georgia came by the gardens today.'

Alan stopped grinning and said a word Daniel thought most appropriate. 'What did she want? She didn't rush tearfully into your arms and beg for a second chance, did she?'

Daniel shook his head. 'No, thank goodness.'

He realised how insensitive that sounded, but Alan understood. He was a guy.

Daniel shifted his hand grip. 'It's over,' he said. 'Maybe it never should have started.'

Alan shrugged. 'I thought you had a good thing going there. All the perks and none of the drama.'

That was what Daniel had thought too, when he'd thought about it at all. That also sounded insensitive, he realised. But he and Georgia had been friends, her work at Kew's millennium seed bank throwing them together occasionally, and somewhere along the line friendship had slipped into something more. At the time he'd hardly noticed it happening.

Normally, he was much more focused about his love life. He'd spot a woman that appealed to him, pick her out from the pack, and then he'd go about pursuing her, changing her mind... Because, if there was one contrary thing about him, it was that he liked the ones that were hard work, took a little chasing. It made the whole thing so much more fun.

But Kelly had been ill, vomiting half the day, and Daniel—apart from being scared out of his wits for his sister—had been thrown in the deep end of caring for two small boys. He supposed all his 'chasing' energy had been tied up elsewhere, and maybe that was why he'd slid into his easy relationship with Georgia.

He'd thought she'd wanted that too. Something with no complications, no dramas. Definitely no wedding rings.

He should have known. If a relationship lasted more than six months, that diamond encrusted time bomb was always there, ticking away in the background. And Daniel knew just how deep that glittery shrapnel could embed itself.

He started climbing again. 'That's not all, though,' he said, glancing at Alan, who was now keeping pace. 'She told me the radio station is holding her to the contract she signed with them.'

Alan looked shocked. 'What? How can they do that? There's no wedding to cover. You said *no*.'

Daniel nodded. 'That's what I said. But, for some unknown reason, she feels the need to reinvent herself, and they're going to follow her around all year while she does it. The *Year of Georgia*, they're calling it.' As if he didn't feel enough of a heel already.

Alan's gift for expletives made itself known again.

But it wasn't really the extra media coverage that warranted such a well-timed word. It was a horrible feeling that, by saying no to Georgia, he'd somehow broken her and now she thought she needed to fix herself.

He scrubbed a hand over his face. This was the very reason he chose women carefully, avoided commitment. He wasn't looking for love and marriage. It was like his pitcher plants—a sticky, sweet-scented trap. Thankfully, unlike a mindless fly, Daniel had a well-developed urge for self-preservation and he usually prided himself on not falling for the lie and getting stuck.

Until Georgia, of course. A mistake he wouldn't make again.

Damn her for seeming so self-sufficient and sensible when underneath she'd been horribly vulnerable. Damn himself for being too caught up in other things to see the truth.

'This thing's never going to end, is it?' he asked Alan as he started off towards the top of the wall with renewed vigour.

Alan shook his head, more in disbelief than in judgement. 'Look on the bright side,' he said as he scrambled to keep up. 'Most men I know would give their right arm to be where you are right now—women flinging themselves at you on a daily basis. It's like shooting fish in a barrel...'

Daniel frowned as he swung a foot into place and pushed himself up over an overhang. He didn't want to shoot fish in a barrel. That was the point!

He didn't want wide-eyed adoration from a woman; she was likely to start wanting more than he was prepared to give. No, he liked to meet a woman on equal terms, play the game, have fun while it lasted and move on.

'Most men you know are bloody idiots, then,' he shouted back at Alan. 'There's interested and then there's desperate and clingy. I know which I prefer.' And then he shot away from his friend and headed for the top of the wall.

As he climbed the burning in his fingertips, in his shoulders and arms, soothed him. He forgot all about radio stations and marriage proposals and bloody Valentine's Day. Instead, he concentrated on the physical sensations of foot meeting wall, fingers grasping hand hold, and after a while a different set of images—a much more appealing set of images—flitted through his brain.

A flash of a hot-pink shoe. The curve of that tight black skirt as it had gone in and out. The glint of the sun on pale blonde hair as it slanted through the conservatory roof. The wry and sexy curve of a pair of crimson lips as she teased him.

That staff pass, twirling gently underneath...

Daniel realised he'd run out of wall. He blinked and looked down. Alan was still struggling with that last overhang.

Hardly surprising his mind had turned to Chloe Michaels. He'd been thinking about that day in the Princess of Wales Conservatory a lot recently. Unfortunately, memories were all he had at the moment, because he'd hardly seen her at all lately. She was like the disappearing woman, always leaving a place just as he arrived.

'Mate,' Alan said, panting. 'If you don't sort out this woman trouble, you're going to finish me off. You've got to let the whole Georgia thing go.'

Daniel nodded. Yes. Georgia. That was the only woman trouble he had at the moment. The only woman trouble he *should* have at the moment.

But that pair of crimson lips was laughing at him, breathing gently in his ear...

He shook his head. *Bad idea, Daniel. Trap that thought and put it on hold.*

He'd just jumped from the frying pan of one relationship—very publicly—and he wasn't planning on landing in another romantic fire right now. He needed to sit back and take stock, give himself some breathing room. He shouldn't be thinking of starting something new, no matter how prettily those little flames danced and invited him in.

He craned his neck to look at the ceiling. It was far too close to his head. He could do with at least another fifty feet of wall to conquer, something to help him shed this restless energy.

'Women are the last thing on my mind at the moment,' he told Alan. 'It's this wall that's the problem. I've climbed it so many times it's easy.'

Alan just grunted.

With one final look at the ceiling, Daniel started to

rappel back down towards the floor. His friend followed suit, matching his pace. 'I need some real rocks to climb. A proper mountain,' Daniel added. 'That's all.'

Twenty minutes later, round the corner in The Railway pub near Kew Gardens station, Alan plopped a full pint glass in front of Daniel at the bar. 'You miss it, don't you?' his friend said. 'Being out in the field?'

Daniel stared at the tiny bubbles swirling and popping on the surface of his beer. His jaw jutted forwards. 'I do,' he replied. Not just the rocks, but the rain on his skin and the wind in his face. The feeling that he was totally free.

'I'm grateful to you for letting me know when this job opened up,' he said. 'But it's just maternity cover, remember? I'll stick it out until your old boss is back. Kelly will be feeling better by then.'

He'd suggested his sister move into his house in Chiswick when she'd split up with her husband; he'd been happy to have someone watching over it when he'd been overseas. Before Madagascar, he'd worked at different bases all over South East Asia, collecting seeds, helping various universities and botanical gardens set up their own seed banks, searching for species that had yet to be named and catalogued.

But then the news had come about Kelly's diagnosis, and he'd come home and moved in himself. There was no way Kelly could have managed through her surgery and chemotherapy without him.

The Head of Tropical Plants job had come up shortly afterwards and he'd jumped at it. The perfect solution while he stayed in London and helped his sister with her two rowdy boys, and while he enjoyed the chance to work closely with his favourite plants, to see if he couldn't produce and name a new variation or two, it had just confirmed to him that Alan was right. This wasn't what he wanted long-term.

'It's been over a year now,' Alan said, 'and Kelly's looking pretty fine to me.'

While Alan's face had been suspiciously blank, there had been a glint of something in his eyes that Daniel didn't like. Instantly, he was on his feet. Much as he liked his college friend, he knew what Alan was like with women. 'Don't you even dare think about my sister that way,' he said. 'She's off-limits.'

Alan held his hands up, palms outwards. 'Whoa there, mate.'

Daniel sat down again. 'Sorry,' he mumbled. Maybe Alan was right about him being on edge about something. He knew he had a bit of a short fuse, but even the *hint* of a spark was setting him off these days. 'She's been through a lot, Al. The last thing she needs right now is more complications.'

'Gee, thanks,' Alan said, his tone full of mock offence. 'That's a very nice way to refer to your oldest mate—a *complication*.'

Daniel's mouth twitched, despite himself. 'You know what I mean.'

Alan just grinned at him. 'Are you sure there's not woman trouble somewhere on the horizon? Other than your over-enthusiastic ex, that is?'

He shook his head. 'No, nothing like that.'

However, an image flashed across his brain: a saucy smile playing on bright red lips, the little wiggle in her hips as she'd walked away...

Alan downed a fair amount of his pint and put his glass back down on the bar. 'In that case, I'd say you really need to get back out to the wilds of God-knows-where again soon.'

Daniel didn't answer. He knew what he wanted, what he ached for, but as *fine* as Kelly looked these days she still tired very easily, and with two small boys to run around after that happened on a fairly regular basis. He reckoned he was here for another six months at the very least.

'I will,' he replied. 'When I can. Besides…I'm trying to write a second book.'

The one he'd been planning for years and finally had time to concentrate on.

His friend just snorted. 'Leave the book for when you're old and grey. In the meantime, you should do something more than rock climbing to blow off steam.' He took another sip of his beer. 'How about deer stalking? One of my father's old friends has invited us on a weekend at his Scottish castle. I can cadge you an invite.'

Daniel shook his head. Holed up in a draughty old castle with some big city businessmen for the weekend? He'd rather let the deer go free and shoot himself. 'Not my kind of thing,' he said firmly.

'Rubbish,' Alan replied. 'We're hunters, you and I. Oh, not in the traditional sense—but you're always after that rare bit of green stuff no one else can locate. It's buried deep in our genetic code, the desire to track and conquer…'

Daniel didn't add that the tendency to become long-winded after only half a pint was also hardwired into Alan's DNA. The best thing to do when his friend got like this was to nod and sip his beer in silence, which was exactly what he did.

Alan made a large gesture with his free hand. 'Men like us, we need the thrill of the chase!'

Daniel gave him a sideways look. 'And when exactly do you hunt?'

Alan blinked. 'I fish,' he said, quite seriously. 'But what I mean is that sitting in that nursery, with all those captive specimens neatly laid out in rows, must be driving you crazy.'

Maybe it was. Because how else could he explain falling into a comfortable relationship with Georgia, of not ending it when he should have? When had he ever been the one to take the path of least resistance? All this tame London living must be lulling him into a coma.

'Don't you worry about me,' he told Alan as he drained the last of his beer. 'I might not be up for tramping through damp heather after a bit of venison, but I'll find something to keep me from going stir crazy. Anyway, there's more than one way of hunting—the plants I work with have taught me that much.'

'Bloody triffids,' Alan said, waving his hand at the barmaid to order another beer. Alan wasn't a fan. He preferred trees. Palms, mostly.

But Daniel could have told him that the majority of insectivorous plants had no moving parts at all. Perhaps, instead of taking his frustration at the currently slow pace of his life out on innocent climbing walls, he should follow their example: be patient, keep still and see what life brought his way.

And since, at the moment, life had brought him a nice cold beer, that was what he intended to concentrate on.

He took another gulp and let the cool liquid run down the back of his throat.

'Holy Moly,' Alan suddenly said, swivelling his head towards the door. He slapped Daniel on the side of his arm to get his attention, and Daniel's nice cold beer sloshed down his front. It seemed that what life gave with one hand it took with the other.

He swatted at the wet patch on his shirt, then looked past Alan to see what all the fuss was about.

Holy Moly was about right.

Chloe Michaels, the disappearing woman, had re-appeared in time for after-work drinks with one of the other women from work—Emma, who was passionate about bamboo and eccentric as they came.

Surprisingly, Chloe doing casual work clothes was every bit as mouth-drying as Chloe Michaels doing smart ones. Those skinny black jeans worked on curves like that—boy, they really did. The ankle-high lace-up boots should have made him think of functional things, like mud and wheelbarrows, but the criss-cross laces brought corsets to mind instead. And then there was the softly clinging grey long-sleeved T-shirt and the leather jacket over the top...

Leather. In his present state of mind that was a very dangerous word.

An itch started, right deep inside him. He suddenly knew that he didn't want to sit back and be patient, see what opportunities life brought his way. He'd spent too long running from the chaos in his life at the moment, letting circumstances chase him. Looking at Chloe Michaels as she glanced round the pub for a seat, her skin fresh, her lips glossy and pink, he knew what he wanted to do.

Alan was right. It was hard-wired into his Y chromosome.

He wanted to hunt.

Chloe's heart had stuttered when she'd walked in the door of The Railway. Damn. She should have known it was a stupid idea to go somewhere so close to the gardens. Because there, not more than fifteen feet away, was Daniel Bradford—or Drop-Dead Daniel, as some of the social media sites were now calling him—hunched over a beer. And he was looking every bit as gorgeous as his new nickname suggested.

Nope, she told herself. *You're finished with that crush.* It'd breathed its last breath ten years ago, and she wasn't planning on resurrecting it. Still, there wasn't any harm in hedging her bets and just keeping out of his way to make sure. She tugged at Emma's sleeve, about to suggest they try the wine bar farther down the smart little parade of shops and cafés, but Daniel chose that moment to turn round.

Their gazes locked, and the heat filling his eyes short-circuited her vocal cords.

It also made her very angry.

His timing really sucked, didn't it? Because if he'd looked at her like that a decade ago she wouldn't be in this mess right now. She might have been in a whole different kind of mess, but at least she wouldn't have been humiliated beyond belief.

'Hi, Daniel!' Now Emma was waving and making her way over to him. Great.

Chloe's plan had been going so well. She'd been effortlessly avoiding Mr *Drop Dead*, but maybe she should have guessed it had all been too easy, that she would have to put her resolve to the test at some point. So she tipped her chin up, smiled and followed Emma towards the bar.

It was at that point she realised Daniel was with someone—a good-looking blond—so she transferred her gaze to him, offered him her smile instead. The grin he returned said he wasn't ungrateful for it.

A dark thundercloud passed across Daniel's expression and settled there. The skin on the backs of Chloe's knees started to tingle and the smile on her face set. She didn't let it drop, though. No need to panic. A quick chat with the two men and she and Emma would be on their way.

She nodded at him. 'Hey there, Indiana.'

A flash of lightning left that thundercloud and zapped her right between the eyebrows.

She left Emma to gush at Daniel while she turned her attention back to the blond. 'Who's your friend?' she asked, slightly disappointed that there was not even a hint of a tickle at the backs of her knees as she met his appreciative gaze, even though this man was every bit as good-looking as his friend.

'You two know each other?' the blond asked incredulously. 'How come you've never introduced us before?' He held out his hand. 'Alan Harrison,' he said, enfolding Chloe's hand in his own, before turning back to Daniel. 'And you call yourself a mate.'

'You've only just got back from Greece,' Daniel muttered. 'She started while you were away.'

Chloe attempted to release her hand, but it seemed Alan wasn't quite ready to let go of it yet. She smiled coolly. 'I'm new at the botanical gardens.'

Alan's eyes widened. 'You're another plant nerd, like us? I'd never have guessed.'

She flinched inwardly at his words, but her smile grew ever brighter on the surface. 'Guilty as charged.' Really guilty. So she'd got a good haircut, learned how to apply liquid eyeliner... Deep inside she was still as much of a plant nerd as she'd ever been.

Alan rested an elbow on the bar and casually looked her up and down. 'You really don't look like one,' he said, a slightly wolfish glimmer creeping into his eyes.

Chloe kept her smile fixed. 'Haven't you heard?' She nodded in Daniel's direction. 'Thanks to your pal there, *plant nerd* is the new *sexy*.'

'Oh, it really is,' Emma said in a breathy rush, looking at Daniel.

Chloe pressed her lips together to stop herself from laughing. Daniel's expression had darkened further, but there was a hint of panic at the backs of his eyes, one she recognised from the day she'd met him hiding from his silver-haired fan club.

But then Daniel looked back at her, and that glint of something changed and warmed. Suddenly, she was the one panicking inside.

She didn't want him to look at her like that, as if he'd like to...

She wasn't going to finish that thought. It was far too X-rated. And far too dangerous.

'What can we get you two ladies to drink?' Alan asked.

Chloe tried to speak, tried to tell him that it was okay, that she and Emma were just going to find a quiet table in the corner and chat about bamboo, but nothing came out. Not quickly enough, anyway.

'Gin and tonic, please,' Emma said loudly.

Chloe didn't have much of a choice now. It would look really rude if she refused. Still, Emma had to be away in half an hour. How bad could it be? She was going to have to work alongside Daniel occasionally. Maybe this would be good practice.

But she made the mistake of catching his eye as she cleared her throat and said, 'White wine would be lovely.' The tingling was back behind her knees, threatening to send rogue messages to her muscles stop keeping her upright and just...*melt*.

Thankfully, a group of people sitting at a table near them got up to leave. Alan stopped leaning on the bar and motioned in its direction. 'Shall we?' He walked over to the table, pulling out a chair for Emma first. Chloe decided she liked him a lot better for that.

She decided it was safer to sit on the same side of the rectangular table as Emma. Alan quickly bagged the seat opposite, which left Daniel no choice but to subject himself to Emma's adoring gaze.

Chloe chuckled to herself while simultaneously breathing a sigh of relief. Emma was doing a very nice job of deflecting the attention from her. She could definitely handle a quick drink with these two men if her colleague kept this up.

In fact, Emma kept Daniel so completely monopolised with her barrage of questions about a new subspecies of bamboo he'd encountered in his previous job that Chloe was free to sit back, sip her wine and listen to a long story Alan was telling about his trip to Corfu.

Every so often she'd glance across at Daniel. He seemed quite happy to answer Emma's queries, but when the other woman smiled and fiddled with her hair his expression remained neutral. When Emma leaned forward across the table, he leaned back. Chloe's amusement at Daniel's expense waned.

She knew what that was like. Knew *just* what it was like.

To want him so badly that you threw everything you had into getting him, letting your mouth run away with you, letting your body language go into overdrive. Emma seemed oblivious, though. She just kept ploughing on.

There was no doubt that she was attractive for her age, but as she talked Chloe just itched to suggest a girls' night in so she could apply serum and a pair of straighteners to that hair. She took a sip of her wine. There were products on the market these days to combat that amount of frizz. If anyone should know, it was Chloe...

Her insides chilled.

There but for the grace of God...

She had not so much a flashback as a flash forward—to who she might have been, had she not subjected herself to that post-graduation makeover.

Stop, she wanted to tell Emma. *Don't do it. He'll push you away, make you feel small and insignificant, not good enough for him.*

She and Emma had chatted enough for her to know that the older woman was unhappily single. Chloe didn't want her to go home that evening after her failed play for Daniel, look in the mirror and decide that if life handed out report cards, the overwhelming verdict would be *could do better*.

Should do better. Must do better.

Chloe knew how much that smarted.

She placed a hand on Emma's arm, grasping at something she'd told her earlier. 'Didn't you say you needed to be out of here at seven-thirty?' she said. 'It's almost that now.'

Well, seventeen minutes past, but who was counting?

Emma paused her interrogation and looked at her watch. 'Oh, cripes! Yes, I almost completely forgot! And I booked this adult education course months ago—the waiting list was huge.' She dragged her eyes from Daniel and sighed. 'I'll have to hear all about Mount Kinabalu another time,' she said, a hint of trailing hopefulness in her voice.

Chloe stood up. 'Come on,' she told Emma, glancing through the vast window that looked over the empty platform. 'The next train is due in a couple of minutes. I'll wait with you.'

'You can't go yet,' Alan said, leaning past her to place a couple of full glasses on the table. 'I got you another wine.' Chloe hadn't even realised he'd left to go to the bar.

Emma glanced between Chloe and Alan and a little smile curved her lips. Chloe started to shake her head. No, she wasn't interested in Alan, and she didn't want Emma's attempt at 'subtle' matchmaking to make him think otherwise. Unfortunately, despite her love of bamboo, it turned out that Emma wasn't very good with sticks—because she'd obviously got the wrong end of this one.

'No, you stay,' her colleague said, grinning at Alan. 'There's no need for you to miss out because of me.'

'Uh—' Chloe didn't get any further with that sentence, because Emma had scooped up her bag and her coat and was heading for the exit.

Alan pressed a full glass of wine into Chloe's hand before calling after the disappearing Emma. '*Another* evening class?' he shouted. 'What is it this time?' then he took another sip of his drink.

Emma stopped and turned in the middle of the room. Chloe could only half see her it was so crowded. 'Pole dancing,' she called back cheerily, and suddenly the whole pub was very quiet. Apart from the sound of Alan softly choking on his beer, of course.

THREE

———

Chloe looked at an equally flabbergasted Daniel and they both burst out laughing. Whether it was at Emma's parting shot or Alan's beer-fuelled snorting from the other side of the table, neither of them really knew. But the urge to giggle subsided quickly when she found herself staring across the table at Daniel Bradford. He wasn't finding the whole thing funny any more, either.

She tugged at the collar of her leather jacket with a finger. Hot. That was what she was finding the whole thing now. Her feet were tingling and her cheeks felt flushed and a delicious warmth was spreading deep inside. And it had nothing to do with the therapeutic effects of having a good laugh.

She swallowed.

Unfortunately, it had everything to do with the not-so-therapeutic effects of staring deep into Daniel Bradford's eyes and wondering what it would be like to kiss him.

She closed her eyes as she took her next sip of wine, breaking the connection.

Nope. Been there, done that, survived the train wreck. Just.

Alan, who had obviously now recovered from his coughing fit, came and sat in the seat beside her and draped a well-toned arm across the back of her chair. 'You're not joining her?'

Chloe had to admire the ego that allowed him to bounce back from having lager spurt out of his nose then continue to flirt as if nothing had happened. She shook her head and nudged her chair further away while pretending she was reaching for her handbag.

'Don't tell me...' Alan said, leaning forward slightly '...you're already proficient?'

This time it was Daniel's turn to choke on his beer.

Too smooth for his own good, Chloe thought as she blinked and looked back at Alan. Still, it didn't worry her. She could handle him. One of the key pieces of reasoning behind the 'new and improved' Chloe was that she'd decided she'd much rather be the kind of woman men ran after than the kind they ran away from. In the intervening decade she'd learned a thing or two about over-enthusiastic suitors—and the disposal thereof.

She just smiled mysteriously and looked away. 'I doubt you'll ever find out.' No point telling him the only poles she was really proficient with were the little green canes she used to support her orchids.

This was her cue to exit. She half stood up and looked at both men in turn. 'Thanks for the drinks, guys, but I really must be going.'

'Must you?' Alan said, half rising from his seat and

sporting what he probably considered was his most appealing smile. Chloe glanced over at Daniel. Once again, her blood danced along in her veins to the beat of bongo drums.

Yep. She really *must* go—before things got totally out of hand.

But then a few things happened in tandem, and she never really got her suitably cool and aloof goodbye out of her mouth. Alan's phone rang and he jumped up, pulled it out of his back trouser pocket and answered it. However, it seemed that Daniel thought Alan was making an ill-advised lunge for her, because he shot to his feet too, eyes flaming, and knocked the table in the process. Chloe's half-finished wine landed in her lap and the glass rolled onto the floor with an almighty crash.

And then Chloe was also on her feet and wine was running down her T-shirt and trousers. Even her boots were wet. She'd be smelling like the back room of an off-licence on the walk home. Most attractive.

Once again, the whole pub had fallen quiet to watch the show. They were certainly getting their money's worth tonight. She pushed past Alan—who was very gallantly continuing his phone conversation—shot a desperate look at Daniel and headed for the door.

From the way her audience's eyes kept switching from her to something behind her, she could tell she was being pursued. She really didn't know what would be worse: to turn round and discover it was Alan, or to turn round and discover it was Daniel, so she just kept weaving through the narrow tables until she could push her way through the crowd to reach the door.

Once outside, she breathed in a mouthful of cold

March air and set off down the street. She lived within walking distance, anyway, and hopefully she'd dry off a little on the way home.

Unfortunately, she wasn't the only one hurrying down the street back towards the gardens. Her pursuer obviously wasn't giving up. She decided to play ignorant. Perhaps, if she pretended she didn't know someone was following her, they might just give up and go away.

It didn't work. And with every step Chloe's blood pressure rose until she thought her curls would stand on end. Eventually, she stopped and spun round so fast her pursuer almost crashed into her.

She was inches from a broad chest. 'What?' she asked it hoarsely.

The chest moved up and down and she could hear him breathing. She must have been walking a lot faster than she'd thought. He didn't say anything, though, so she tilted her eyeballs upwards until she could see that it was Daniel Bradford staring back down at her.

He held up one of the little bar towels that all good pubs had stocked away somewhere. 'You had wine on your jacket,' he said gruffly.

'Oh.' She stared at him.

He was still holding up the towel. She was still not taking it.

Slowly, and with surprising gentleness, he took the towel and dabbed at the drips on her left arm, which had now run from biceps to wrist. When he picked up her hand to clean up her cuff, she stopped breathing. From the eerie silence in the dark street, she realised he had too. Simultaneously, they both stopped looking at her sleeve and looked at each other.

Go on, an evil little voice on her shoulder whispered. *Pucker up and launch yourself at him again. It might work this time.*

No!

No. She'd seen the way he'd looked at Emma that evening. How could she be thinking of taking it one step further? Did she have a strange psychotic illness no one had ever diagnosed? *Bradforditis.* One look at the man and she was all sorts of crazy.

She wriggled her hand out of his grasp, almost whimpering as the pads of his fingers brushed the soft underside of her wrist, and stepped away.

'Thank you,' she said, folding her arms across her chest as best she could. With the engineering marvel of a bra she was wearing, it wasn't easy. 'This is my favourite jacket.'

Daniel stepped forward. 'Look...about Alan...'

She raised a hand, held him at bay. 'No need. I'm quite used to taking care of myself. He didn't offend me.'

'When you ran out—'

She shook her head, cutting him off. Why *had* she run out? 'I just...decided I'd rather clean up without an audience,' she said. 'Any more drama from our table and someone would have stood up in the corner and started selling ice creams.'

And then Daniel Bradford spoiled all her attempts at backing off and being sophisticated by crinkling up his pale green eyes and smiling at her.

Ping!

Yep. She was pretty sure another thread of her sanity had just snapped.

'*Do* you fancy an ice cream?' he said softly, still smiling.

Chloe let her arms drop by her sides. 'You know what?' she said. 'I really do.'

'Come on.' He led her a few shops down to the little express supermarket that was still open. Once inside he strode over to the tiny freezer containing ice creams and slid the lid open. 'Take your pick.'

She chose a decadent one: two layers of chocolate with caramel trapped between. Daniel grabbed something plainer. And once he'd paid they walked out of the shop, quickly rid the ice creams of their wrappers and walked down the street in silence, only the cracking of thin chocolate and the slurping of ice cream could be heard.

'Thank you,' she said, when they reached the end of the short parade of shops and stopped by an old horse trough, now filled with daffodils. 'For the ice cream and the mop up job.'

He shrugged. 'No problem.'

He was staring at her lips again. Chloe's heart began to pound, but Daniel lifted a finger to the edge of his own mouth, not hers. 'You've got a bit of...'

Pulse still thudding in her ears, she shot out her tongue and captured a bit of stray caramel that had stuck to the corner of her lip. Daniel Bradford seemed to be very interested in the process. In fact, he seemed to be leaning in closer to get a better look.

Run.

Don't think about it, just run.

Ah. That must be the angel sitting on the opposite shoulder from the other little voice. About time it showed up and offered some sensible advice.

He cleared his throat, looked down intently at her. 'I know this is a bit back to front, that we've just had what could be considered dessert...'

She licked her lips again. More out of nervousness than because of stray caramel.

'But why don't we round it all up by having a starter and a main course somewhere else?' He smiled again, and Chloe discovered the caramel had travelled to her knees.

Oh, it was so tempting...

This was what she'd fantasised about, aged nineteen, on many a night in her student digs—Daniel Bradford, looking at her this way, asking her in that deep, earthy voice of his if they could go somewhere alone together.

She shook her head, and just that motion helped the next words out. 'I'm not sure that's a good idea...We're colleagues. People will talk...and I want to get on at Kew because of what I can do,' she said quietly, 'not because people think I'm sleeping with the boss.'

His lips curved into the sexiest of smiles, telling her that he had an answer for that one. 'There's no rule against it,' he said. 'And we don't have to broadcast it. It'll be our secret.'

She shook her head. 'With the attention you're generating right now that's nigh on impossible.'

She was a genius for coming up with that one! It was perfect.

He nodded, pressed his lips together in grim acceptance. 'I can understand that. My life is a bit of a circus at present. But maybe later, when all the fuss has died down?'

Chloe knew she must be earning brownie points with someone somewhere, because she found the strength to shake her head again, her curls gently moving side to side.

'Sorry, Indiana. Thank you, though… It was very sweet of you to ask.'

And then she turned and walked away, leaving him staring after her.

It should have felt like a victory.

Daniel marched the half mile from the Princess of Wales conservatory to the tropical nurseries in record time the following morning. He wasn't in a good mood.

He passed The Orangery restaurant and headed up the main path towards the kids' play area, then slipped through an iron gate next to the café and left the public area of the gardens behind in favour of the relative sanctuary of the propagation and research greenhouses.

A soursop tree was due to arrive this morning, part of a trade with the botanical gardens in St Lucia, and Daniel wanted to see the specimen for himself. Alan was standing back and supervising while a couple of horticultural students moved the waxy-leafed tree with its spiky fruit from a trolley onto the floor. He turned round when he heard Daniel approaching.

'You okay?' he said.

Daniel gave him a weary, having-one-heck-of-a-day nod. 'Yup.'

A couple of people had asked him exactly the same

thing this morning. Why did they keep doing that? It was most strange.

Alan issued a couple of final instructions to the students before shooing them away. When the two lads were gone and the sliding door of the nursery was closed, he turned to look at his boss.

'There's something you need to see.' He gave Daniel a hooded look and pulled his smartphone from his back pocket. 'I thought you needed to know before it goes viral.'

He punched a couple of buttons then twisted the phone round to show Daniel the screen. Daniel swore loudly and fluently, then snatched the phone from Alan's hand. Unfortunately, seeing it up close and staring hard at it didn't make the Internet news headline go away.

Valentine's man finally trapped? it screamed, and underneath it was a picture of him and Chloe, obviously taken the night before, although he'd had no idea anyone had been walking past with a mobile phone to capture the moment. It must have been when he'd been wiping the wine off Chloe's jacket, a very innocent pastime, he'd have thought, but this photo showed him holding her wrist and they were staring at each other, lost to everyone else. Chloe's lips were parted and he was leaning in slightly, making it look as if he were about to kiss her.

Daniel closed his eyes and handed the phone back to his friend before opening them again.

'This isn't what it looks like,' he said.

Alan just shrugged. 'I knew the minute she walked

in the door that you were toast. Can't blame a guy for trying, though.'

Well, at least Alan was being philosophical about it. 'Who's seen this?'

Alan pressed his lips together and shook his head. 'Not sure. The girls in the café had been cooing over it for half an hour when I stumbled upon them.'

Just when he thought his crazy life was getting back to normal.

'So...what's the story with Miss Fancy Knickers?' Alan said, smiling a little.

Daniel forgot to look cross. 'Who?' he asked, genuinely confused.

'That's the nickname some of the students coined for Miss Orchid House.' He held up his hands. 'It's not that I don't appreciate the view, but those shoes and skirts she wears some days are hardly practical wear for a job like ours, even if she is just messing around with flowers instead of digging beds.' He leaned forward and lowered his voice. 'So...*are* they?'

Daniel's voice was low and warning. 'Are they what?'

Alan's smile upgraded itself into a lascivious grin. 'Fancy.'

'Not you too!' Daniel turned and pulled the sliding door open. 'I believe the official phrase is: *No comment*,' he said just before he slammed it closed again.

He strode away. A couple of the nursery team ducked for cover. Just as well, really. They'd obviously worked out that he was liable to assign the grottiest jobs to anyone who got in his way when he was feeling like this. And, with having to watch Kelly struggling through her chemo for months on end, there had been plenty of days when he'd been in a mood like this.

Fancy knickers. Humph.

No chance of him finding that out at present. He'd barely touched her, let alone got on first name terms with her underwear. And just thinking about said underwear was making it very difficult to calm down.

And it would have to be 'no comment' if anyone else asked him about Chloe, because he wasn't about to tell anyone he'd asked her out and she'd turned him down. That would be too humiliating.

Like what you did to Georgia.

No. That wasn't the same. Georgia had gone live on air and made the choice to publicise her ill-advised proposal. That hadn't been his fault at all. He'd asked Chloe out in private, just the two of them. Or so he'd thought.

Still, if he was feeling a fraction of the mortification Georgia had felt on Valentine's Day, it was no wonder it had taken her a month before she'd been able to face him in person. That must have been the pits.

Oh, heck.

Georgia.

He had a pretty good idea she hadn't seen this yet, and when she did she was going to kill him. He'd been able to tell from her expression yesterday that she was still feeling raw, even if she agreed that ending it had been the best thing for both of them.

To Georgia it would look as if he'd taken her visit yesterday to go out and bed the nearest available hottie. It didn't help to know he'd been on that train of thought himself last night, hardly stopping to think how it might look to anyone else. And Georgia had always had a bit of a thing about women like Chloe...

Oh, bloody hell. *Chloe.*

When Georgia was finished with him, Chloe would bring him back to life and make him suffer a second time. What a mess.

He yanked the greenhouse door open and strode out into the fresh air. There was only one thing to do: he had to talk to both of them before they found out about it from anyone else.

The morning had been a hectic one and Chloe decided to go and sit on a bench to eat her lunch. While it was cold enough to still need her coat, it was the best kind of day March could deliver, and she was determined to mop up as much sun as she could.

She'd always wanted to work at Kew, ever since she'd trained here. It was the most amazing place in the world as far as she was concerned. And who wanted to hide away in an office or a staff tearoom when there were acres of beautiful gardens on their doorstep?

An empty bench was waiting for her just away from one of the main paths. She made her way to it and sat down, trying to let the tranquillity seep into her, but she hardly took in the carpet of lilac-blue crocuses or the swathes of daffodils covering some of the sloping banks, because her mind was too busy living the events of the night before.

Half of her was screaming at the other half for having walked away from Daniel, and the other half congratulated itself on being safe and sensible. While the two continued to have a tug of war inside her skull, she

closed her eyes and let her head slip back, enjoying the
sun on her face.

She wasn't sure how long she stayed like that, but the
snap of a twig nearby disturbed her. She sat up quickly
and opened her eyes. Her heart had started to pump a
little faster when she'd heard that noise and now she
knew why. Indiana Jones, minus his secateurs, had come
to pay her a visit.

She snapped the lid back on her salad and looked him
evenly in the eye. That was the sort of thing New Chloe
did. That girl wasn't scared of anything.

However, for the first time in years she was aware
of another presence at the fringes of her consciousness.
Deep down inside, another Chloe—the naive frizzy
mouse—was huddled in a corner, twitching.

No, she thought. *That sad, geeky girl is dead. Something
far better has risen from her ashes.* She clamped down
hard on the ghostly presence. That was all it was. A
memory. An echo.

'Don't suppose you have another ice cream on you?'
she asked, closing her eyes again briefly. 'It's more the
weather for it today.'

He shook his head and silently pulled a smartphone
with a large screen from his pocket. 'I'm sorry,' he said
as he handed it to her. 'This isn't anywhere near as nice
as ice cream.'

Chloe scrolled through the whole blog entry carefully, reading every word. It was the picture that did
the most damage, though. In the grainy photograph
she was looking up at Daniel as he leant towards her,
her eyes wide, her lips...waiting.

She handed the phone back to him without saying

anything, not wanting to see it any more. She must have made a face, because he shook his head and then said, 'You've every right to be upset.'

It wasn't that. She wasn't upset that people thought she was romantically involved with Daniel Bradford. It might make her life at Kew a little more complicated, sure, but it was hardly anything to get her knickers in a twist about. No, what she was really worried about was that photograph.

'How many people have seen this?' she asked, looking straight ahead, eyes fixed on the Georgian orangery that now served as the gardens' main restaurant.

She heard the fragments of pine cones and twigs beneath his feet crunch as he shifted his weight. 'There's no way of knowing, but I think we have to assume *everyone*.'

Chloe nodded. Okay. She could cope with this. People might see the picture, but they wouldn't recognise it, wouldn't know what it meant.

She turned her head to look at him, made her cheek muscles tighten to pull the corners of her lips upwards. Then she shifted along the bench and made room for him. He blinked, confusion etched into his features, and sat down.

He was probably expecting a scene. Lots of women did scenes. Luckily for him, New Chloe had banished them from her life. She only did confident and breezy and unfazed.

'So...what do we do now?' she asked, leaning back and feigning a relaxed posture.

He stared intently at her for a moment. 'That's up

to you,' he said. 'I could contact the blog, make a statement...'

Chloe thought for a moment. 'No...I don't think it's worth it.'

Unfortunately, the old adage was true: pictures did speak louder than words, and that one of her and Daniel was gabbling uncontrollably, contradicting any carefully worded denial they could come up with. There was no point.

'Are you sure?' The closed, slightly guarded look he'd been giving her softened. Chloe nodded brightly. She didn't want his concern, didn't want to see any more flashes of that warm, more caring side she'd just glimpsed of Daniel Bradford. Things were hard enough as it was.

She stood up and walked a little bit before turning back to face him. 'It'd be like shouting into the wind. People will think what they want to think, no matter what we say.'

Daniel scowled. 'We can't just sit back and do nothing.'

She shook her head. 'I didn't say we should do nothing. I just said we shouldn't bother contacting the press to deny it. We don't have to go on the offensive to beat this thing.'

He looked at her as if she were speaking a foreign language. To Daniel Bradford, she probably was. She smiled. Properly this time.

She walked over to him, slid the phone from his hand without touching his fingers and showed him the picture. 'It's not as if we're in a full lip-lock,' she said, ignoring the shiver that ran up her spine at the thought. 'It's innocent enough. I think we should just ignore it, go on as normal. People will soon realise there's nothing in it.'

Daniel took the phone back from her, and this time their fingers did touch. And the way his eyes lit up, she guessed it wasn't entirely an accident. She pulled her hand away and stuffed it in her coat pocket, where it continued to tingle.

'No comment?'

'No comment,' she agreed. 'Perfect. That's exactly what people say in circumstances like this.'

Daniel stood up. 'You're saying you just want to ride whatever comes, ignore it?'

She nodded again. She was good at ignoring things.

Daniel shook his head as he put the phone back in his pocket.

'You haven't given an interview since Valentine's Day, have you?' she asked.

'No...' He looked away and then back at her. He was still frowning, but now she could tell he was turning her idea over instead of just resisting it. 'I suppose you're right. Starting a dialogue may just increase the frenzy.'

Chloe walked forward, sat down on the bench and picked up her salad box again. 'Great. All sorted,' she said, unclipping the lid.

Daniel stared at her, brow still furrowed. He seemed on the verge of saying something, but he finally said, 'I'd better go and give Alan back his phone.'

She smiled back and waved her fork slightly before popping a cherry tomato in her mouth and swallowing it almost whole. 'Well, if Alan is as addicted to his smartphone as I am to mine, you'd better hurry. He may already be having withdrawal symptoms.'

Daniel gave a wry smile and stared at the phone, as if he couldn't quite believe in the seductive pull in that little bit of technology. 'I appreciate you being understanding about this,' he said as he put it back in his pocket.

'No problem,' she said, managing to sound fairly normal, although she was fairly sure that tomato had lodged itself somewhere in her throat. 'And if Alan is shaking and sweating when you get back to him, I recommend an early lunch break. Half an hour of Vengeful Ducks should get him back on track.'

'Let me thank you somehow,' Daniel said, lowering his voice, and an irresistible little glimmer of naughtiness twitched his mouth into an off-centre smile. 'How about dinner?'

Chloe blinked slowly and licked her lips. 'I thought we talked about this last night,' she said, looking at her salad and using her fork to tease a bit of carrot.

When she looked back up at Daniel he was still smiling at her. It took all she had not to fling her salad to one side and have him for lunch instead.

'Can't blame a guy for trying,' he said, then nodded and headed back towards the nurseries.

When he was out of earshot Chloe let go of her intercostal muscles and allowed the coughing fit she'd been holding back to take over. Eventually, the tomato made its way down the right hole.

She put her salad box down on the bench beside her, put her elbows on her knees and rested her face in her hands. She really didn't want to go back to who she'd been when she'd first met Daniel. That Chloe had been a nice enough girl, the class swot, always excelling at everything. She hadn't cared that she hadn't followed the latest fashion trends or had only a passing acquaintance with the opposite sex. Because that Chloe had known that everything came easy to her, that she'd hardly ever had to try to be good at anything.

And then Daniel Bradford had walked into her life and had shown her exactly where she'd been lacking.

She hadn't realised she wasn't any good at being a girl until he'd come along. And that was a pretty important thing when you were one.

For a girl who'd never failed at anything, crashing and burning so spectacularly in the male-female stakes had come not just as a shock, but a reality slap. That was what the grown-up world was all about. And nice-but-geeky Chloe just hadn't been cutting it.

She couldn't have that.

Right from an early age her parents had pushed their rather precocious only child to excel, to be the best at everything she did. So how had she failed at something so basic, something that was supposed to come naturally?

She drew in a breath and sat up. It didn't matter any more. She'd fixed it. Now being not just a girl, but a woman, was something Chloe Michaels got top marks in, so she really shouldn't worry.

A wisp of breeze curled itself around her, lifted a strand of hair and pushed it across her face. She brushed it aside. There was no point in dwelling on the past—she had a problem in the present that needed fixing.

Unfortunately, the root was the same: Daniel.

What was she going to do about him, about this stupid article?

Ignore it, she told herself firmly. *That's what you've got to do. Ignore the stupid blog. Ignore the way Indiana there makes your skin tighten and your pulse zing. Most of all, ignore that horrible photograph.*

A cold feeling spiked through Chloe and she masked it by sitting up and spearing another vegetable, chewing it quickly then swallowing it fast.

Yes, ignore the fact that, despite the trademark blonde curls and the red lips, she hadn't recognised herself in that photo. Not the version of herself she was today, anyway.

Because, in the grainy greyness of that mobile phone picture, it hadn't been 'new and improved' Chloe staring up at Daniel all wide-eyed and breathy; it had been the Mouse.

FOUR

———

Daniel caught a flash of colour out of the corner of his eye as he flicked a paintbrush full of pollen over a plant he was trying to propagate. Instinctively, he swung round to find it again.

Just a brightly coloured plastic bag one of the staff had walked past the door of his nursery with. Not a pink shoe, or an emerald blouse or even a pair of smiling ruby lips.

He stood up and scrubbed a hand over his face.

He was losing it, wasn't he?

Just a hint of colour, which he now seemed to associate with Chloe, because everyone else here wore variations of brown and green and navy blue, or a scent like her perfume—an easy mistake to make in a greenhouse full of flowers—and he'd react. He'd seek first and think later, making him just like the insects who were lured by the smell and hue of the plant he was tending. They couldn't help it.

He couldn't help it.

Another dash of soft pink at the edge of his peripheral vision. He turned immediately, then swore.

This time it was Chloe, popping her head in the door of one of the other rooms and asking one of the horticultural students something. She was wearing a top that clung in all the right places. She smiled at the two young men, was charming and poised. Just as she was with him. No difference.

No difference at all.

It was driving him mad.

He'd tried everything, every trick up his sleeve—every look, every line—and she was still completely unaffected.

He bowed his head and turned his attention back to the bulbous *Nepenthes hamata* he was working on. Most people thought of plants as pretty things, but this specimen was dark and fierce-looking. He thought it was beautiful, but with vicious-looking black teeth round the opening of the pitcher it resembled something out of a science-fiction movie more than a bloom fit for a bridal bouquet.

He was trying to cross it with another species that was a deep purply-black. If he succeeded, he'd have a plant that would give even Sigourney Weaver nightmares.

He glanced up again, but realised he was subconsciously searching for soft pink, and made himself focus on the plant instead.

Not her. This plant wouldn't scare her. In fact, nothing seemed to rattle her, and he both admired and resented that ability. Chloe Michaels was like her own unique subspecies of womankind. Bred to resist him.

And, with all the lurid rumours flying round about them, her apathy just rubbed salt into the wound. Maybe it was just stubbornness on his part, an unwillingness to admit defeat?

A fly buzzed round the *Nepenthes,* alighting on the slippery edge of the plant's mouth and climbing inside. Daniel knew that was the last he'd see of it. The waxy interior would prevent any escape.

He studied the plant once again. So beautiful, but so deadly, luring most unwitting insects in with the promise of sweetness but the reality of slow drowning and digestion.

He heard heels on the concrete floor, sensed a patch of pink walk past his nursery door, but, despite the urge to turn, he kept his eyes trained on the shiny black teeth at the gaping mouth of the pitcher.

Maybe he would do well to learn a lesson from that fly.

Emma slid into the empty chair next to Chloe in the Orangery restaurant. It was a bright May afternoon, temperatures approaching those of high summer.

'So...' Emma said, leaning in close and lowering her voice. 'How are things going between you and the gorgeous Daniel?'

Chloe stopped chewing. If she had to say the equivalent of *no comment* just one more time she thought she'd scream. Even if it had been her clever idea.

'There's nothing to tell,' she said, after swallowing her mouthful.

Emma just grinned at her. When the rumours about her and Daniel had first surfaced Emma had given her a wide berth, but now she'd decided to buddy up with Chloe and live vicariously through her colleague's fictitious love life.

'I know that's the *official* line,' Emma said, her eyes gleaming over the top of her soup bowl, 'but everybody knows there's more to it than that. Come on...just one juicy detail...*please*?'

Chloe's eyebrows raised. 'Everybody? Still?'

'Pretty much,' Emma said as she slurped butternut squash soup off her spoon.

Chloe stared at her sandwich in dismay. She'd hardly seen Daniel in the last few weeks, let alone spoken to him. This 'deny everything' tactic had given her the perfect excuse to keep her distance.

'I don't know how you're managing to be so discreet,' Emma added between mouthfuls, so enthusiastic she dribbled a big glob of orange soup down her front. 'If I owned a man like that, I wouldn't be able to keep my hands off him—at home *or* at work.'

Chloe closed her eyes. It didn't matter what they did, did it? They were damned if they did and damned if they didn't. Keeping their distance, only nodding at each other in hallways when they passed, was just as much a confirmation of a steamy relationship as if they'd stripped naked and done it in the middle of the Palm House.

But it had worked. Media attention on Daniel and his ex had lulled. Thanks to that blog article, Daniel wasn't The One Who Got Away any more; he was The One Who'd Been Snared. Nowhere near as appealing. The women of London were moving on to pastures new.

'How's the pole dancing going?' she asked Emma, and thankfully her friend took the bait.

'The course finished and I've switched to belly dancing. You should try it!'

And as Emma gushed on about her new hobby an idea solidified in Chloe's head.

She would go and talk to Daniel, suggest they end this *no comment* nonsense. She felt as if invisible ropes, projected by other people's minds, were tying the pair of them together, each day becoming tighter and tighter, and it was making her itchy. It was time to break free.

And, thankfully, since Alan had also mentioned that the carnivorous plant display in the Princess of Wales Conservatory was being updated today, she knew just where to find him.

When Chloe entered the Wet Tropics zone of the Princess of Wales Conservatory she almost bumped into a woman in a raincoat standing at the slope that led down to the lily-pad pool.

'Sorry,' she said, but the woman didn't hear her. She was too busy staring at something on the other side of the pond. Chloe followed her gaze and quickly worked out why. Not bothering to wait for a ladder or any other suitable piece of equipment, Daniel had climbed outside the railing of the stepped walkway that led from the pond's edge over the water to the upper level. His attempts to hook a recently planted basket of trailing pitchers from a chain suspended from the ceiling were drawing quite a crowd.

Chloe folded her arms and enjoyed the view. She knew he relished finding plants in inaccessible places, particularly mountainsides, and he seemed totally at home hanging off the walkway, his feet pressing down onto the edge of the concrete path and the taut muscles of his outstretched left arm gripping onto the railing. His T-shirt stretched tight across his back and when he leaned a little bit further, exposing a band of tanned skin between hem and belt, there was a collective female sigh from the crowd of onlookers.

Chloe almost joined in herself. This was what had attracted her to him in the first place as an impressionable young student. Not just the good looks, but his passion for his area of study, the way he flung himself wholeheartedly into everything.

She frowned. While present-day Daniel obviously still liked a physical challenge, if she compared him to the Daniel she'd crushed over in her student days she realised there were subtle differences too. A decade ago he'd smiled more, laughed more. Present-day Daniel seemed more tense, more self-contained. Less...happy.

The woman next to her made a funny noise. Chloe turned to look at her. 'Are you okay?'

'Oh, yes,' the woman replied emphatically, her eyes still fixed on Daniel. 'Just getting up my nerve.'

Chloe stared at her for a second and began to walk quickly towards the crowd by the pool. A strange tickling under her skin told her she needed to get to him, and she needed to get to him fast. As she neared the pool he disappointed the sighing onlookers by finishing his task and hopping back over the railing to stand on the walkway. The round of applause he received took him completely by surprise.

She was just trying to fight the tide of the dispersing crowd when the woman she'd bumped into earlier dashed past her and ran up the ramp towards Daniel. He was facing the other direction but he must have heard her approach, because when she was within a few feet of him he turned round.

The woman skidded to a halt, fiddled with the buttons of her raincoat, then ripped the flaps open.

Chloe pushed her way through the onlookers and ran up the ramp behind her. Even from that vantage point she could see there was way too much bare skin under that coat. Daniel just stared at the woman, eyes on stalks. And not in a good way.

Everything stopped. The only thing moving was Chloe and the only noise was the overhead misters, hissing their displeasure. Exactly why she was racing to Daniel's side she wasn't sure; she just knew she had to do something.

When she reached the woman, she noted—thank goodness—that it wasn't as bad as she'd first feared. At least she was wearing a set of sexy black lingerie... and a message, written on what looked like permanent marker on her torso.

I do, Daniel, it read. *Do you?*

He just stared at the writing, a look of frozen horror on his face.

Chloe stared too, unable to work out just what kind of desperation drove a woman to do something like that, but then her gaze drifted from midriff to face. What she saw there was possibly even more shocking.

Not just desperation but longing.

The same kind of longing she'd seen in the mirror all those years ago when she'd first met Daniel. The agitation she'd felt while she'd been pushing her way through the crowd quickly turned to sympathy.

'I...I...' Daniel managed to stutter, and suddenly Chloe knew exactly what she had to do.

She hitched the fallen raincoat from round the woman's elbows and draped it across her shoulders, then she went to stand beside Daniel. After taking a deep breath, she slid her fingers into his.

He did a good job of hiding his flinch of surprise, and a second later his larger, stronger hand closed firmly around hers.

The woman's slightly glazed expression melted into one of horror. 'You're...you're the girl in the picture,' she said, her voice high and wavering, 'on that website...'

Chloe nodded and moved close to Daniel, pressing herself into his side. 'Yes,' she said. 'Sorry.'

The woman nodded and clutched the coat around herself. 'Oh, God,' she muttered. 'I feel so stupid.'

Chloe stepped forward, but it seemed Daniel was reluctant to let go of her hand. He still hadn't moved and his jaw was set in a hard line. She shot him a *work with me* look and he unclenched his hand enough to let her wiggle her fingers free.

She put her arm around the woman and led her further along the walkway, high above the Wet Tropics zone and through a glass door into another section, away from the staring crowd.

'I'm so sorry,' the woman said. 'I saw that picture of you two online, but there'd never been anything more. I didn't realise you two... I thought he was available.'

'It's okay,' Chloe said softly. 'I understand. He...he has this weird effect on people. On women.'

He certainly had a weird effect on Chloe.

Tears slid from between the woman's lashes. She nodded and looked at the floor. 'He just looked like... seemed to be...I don't know...the kind of man who'd really know how to look after a woman.' Her head jerked up. 'Is he?' she asked, slightly desperately, her fierce gaze demanding Chloe made eye contact.

Chloe didn't know what to say to that. She hardly knew Daniel, not really. And the truth was she'd been on the receiving end of one of the most humiliating and mortifying moments of her life at his hand. She certainly hadn't felt very special or looked after at that moment.

But this woman didn't need to hear that, and there was something in the tone of her question that begged for something positive to cling to from this whole sorry experience.

Chloe spotted a couple of the Kew constabulary slowly making their way towards them. She didn't know what experiences this woman had had with the opposite sex to get herself in this state, but they couldn't have been good ones. Maybe she just needed to know that all men weren't rats, that there were some good ones out there.

She thought about the way Daniel tended his plants, how gentle and patient he could be. Now, if he could bring some of that into his personal life, he really would be a catch. It wasn't too much of a stretch to give the right answer. She met the woman's gaze.

'Yes, he is,' she said quietly. And as the two constables reached them she reached down and squeezed the woman's hand.

'I think she might just need a strong cup of tea and a sympathetic ear,' she told the constables. 'No harm done.'

The female officer of the pair smiled and nodded, and Chloe let out a breath. She really hoped the poor woman would get the help she needed.

As for Chloe? Well, maybe she was in need of a little help herself.

No harm done. Really?

She wasn't so sure about that.

Because she knew that by her actions a few moments ago she'd announced to the onlookers, including Kew staff, and maybe even to the whole world—via the considerate people who'd silently recorded the whole episode on their smartphones—that she and Daniel Bradford were a couple.

The crowd, who were far too nosey to disperse, watched along with Daniel as Chloe re-entered the Wet Tropics zone and walked back towards him. Her chin was high and her make-up perfect. She looked so in control, so assured...

So different from that crazy woman in the raincoat.

The contrast soothed his soul.

At least, it did until she was right in front of him. Just as she reached him he saw a flicker of something else behind the perfection, something in her eyes as she looked up at him—uncertainty, blended with a pinch of nerves.

That shook him.

For weeks now she'd had him convinced that she was impervious, iron-clad. Chloe Michaels was merely a delectable package he was itching to unwrap. A prize to be won. So it was a shock to be reminded that she was a real woman, one maybe, that still had all the idiosyncrasies and puzzling insecurities they seemed to be pre-programmed with.

But then the *something* he'd seen was gone, and she was back to normal—all gloss and glamour. All colour and scent. He breathed out, relieved that she'd tucked whatever it was he'd seen away, out of reach, and he didn't need to worry about it any more.

He didn't say anything to her, just closed the distance between them, caught her hand in his, then led her out of the Princess of Wales Conservatory.

Once outside they kept walking, still joined, far away from the glasshouse, up the Broadwalk and on. They stopped briefly by the lake in front of the vast Palm House.

'We need to talk,' he said, 'about what just happened back there.'

She nodded.

'Somewhere private,' he added.

They turned their heads in unison and looked at the Victorian marvel of curved white iron and thin panes of glass not more than a hundred feet away. Although it was one of the prime visitor spots at Kew, and unlikely to be empty, it was filled with drooping plants and massive leaves. Daniel knew there were plenty of places to hide if one knew where to go.

Once inside, he ignored the 'No Entry' sign at the bottom of one of the ornate spiral staircases that led from the floor of the Palm House to the gallery that ringed the dome. 'They've just finished trimming the giant bamboo,' he explained, 'so we should be the only ones up here for now.'

Chloe nodded and let him pull her up the stairs, unable to say anything sensible. She'd been fine while the whole drama had been unfolding back in the Princess of Wales Conservatory, cool as the proverbial cucumber, but now, as the damp heat of the tropical greenhouse seeped beneath her clothes and moistened her skin, she couldn't stop thinking about the woman in the raincoat.

The way the crowd had looked at her, with a mixture of curiosity and disgust... The poor woman had seemed so lost and desperate. How had she not known that what she was about to do would be a horrible mistake?

The heels of Chloe's boots clanged on the scrollwork metal steps and she shifted her weight so she was treading on the balls of her feet. She felt as if she'd left her stomach on the iron-grated floor below them. The air grew hotter and wetter, making it hard to gulp it in as she climbed.

Ten years ago, was that how Daniel had seen her? Had he felt that same mix of revulsion and pity? She shivered at the thought.

They'd reached the top of the curling staircase and she paused, taking in a steadying breath before following Daniel down the narrow gallery until they were almost completely hidden from view by a giant palm and a bushy cannonball tree.

Daniel turned and looked at her.

Yes, this was the expression she wanted to see on his face. Not a hint of revulsion. Slighty perplexed, if anything, because he'd lost that perpetual frown and his expression was the most open she'd ever seen it.

'Thank you for what you did back there. I had no idea how to handle that gracefully. After Georgia...I just didn't want to say the wrong thing.'

Chloe couldn't help but smile, just a little. Hanging off bridges and scaling mountains were what Daniel Bradford was graceful at. The interpersonal stuff, not so much.

He shook his head. 'This whole thing, ever since that stupid radio show, has been crazy.'

'I'm hoping today's particular manifestation was a one-off,' Chloe said, feeling less scorn for the woman than was coming out in her voice. For some reason, she didn't want Daniel to know that she'd identified with the poor soul at all.

He shook his head, looked away for a second, and the tug on her hand as his weight shifted reminded her he hadn't let go of it. She should step back, make it look natural, but she should break contact.

She should. But she didn't.

'I don't know how I'm going to take nine more months of this.'

'Nine months?' She wrinkled her brow. 'I didn't realise there was a set timescale for Valentine's-related insanity. Or an expiry date.'

One corner of his mouth twisted. 'No, it's not that. I'm getting out of here—going on the expedition with the South Asia team. Early next spring I'll be back in Borneo and all this so-called civilisation will only be a distant nightmare.'

Nine months? Chloe didn't like the way her chest squeezed at that thought.

'It'll die down,' she said.

He frowned. 'That's what I thought at first but, if anything, it's getting worse.'

'I heard your ex on the radio yesterday,' she said, 'doing her monthly spot about her bounce-back year.'

Daniel looked thunderous. 'I can't really hold it against her—the radio station is making her do it—but it's the broadcasting equivalent of a full moon. Brings out all the crazies...' His expression softened. 'You helped, though. That woman backed off when she thought we were together.'

Chloe nodded. 'I guess the cat's out of the bag—even if it was an illusory bag and an illusory cat. *No comment* isn't going to cut it now.'

He gave her an uneven smile. 'If today was anything to go by, *No comment* wasn't cutting it anyway.'

There was that.

She sighed and gently slid her hand out of his. He didn't stop her. Then she turned and rested her forearms on the gallery rail and stared out over the Palm House, even though, because of the secluded spot they'd chosen, much of what she could see was the dark waxy leaves of the bushy tree in front of her. It was so hot up here. Her jumper was starting to cling and her fringe was growing damp against her forehead.

'So what do you want to do about it?' he asked, then leant on the rail beside her, mirroring her pose.

For a long time neither of them said anything but, eventually, a seed of an idea dropped into Chloe's brain from somewhere, floating on the wind. A few minutes later it had grown into a little green shoot of a plan, new and fresh and unexpected. She didn't want to see any more women suffering the way that lady had today.

And she didn't think Daniel deserved the embarrassment, either.

She pushed her weight back onto her feet and straightened. 'Let's make it work for us,' she said.

He turned to look at her, clearly unconvinced that was possible. 'How?'

She took a deep breath. Her heart began to pump faster. *This must be what it feels like for them*, she thought, *for the guys, when they're gathering up the courage to ask a girl out.*

But this wasn't like that. Not really. Because she wasn't really asking him out; she certainly wouldn't risk being refused by Daniel a second time.

So she swallowed her nerves down, then looked him in the eye. 'I have a proposal for you.'

FIVE

——

Alarm filled Daniel's eyes. Chloe could practically hear the word *proposal* ringing round his head. He was feeling panicked? Good. At least that meant they were on even ground now.

'Not that kind of proposal,' she added wearily.

Daniel folded his arms across his chest and leaned back on the opposite railing, close to the curved glass of the Palm House's roof. 'What do you mean, then?'

Chloe swallowed. 'Have dinner with me,' she said, her heart pumping. 'Or something else. Once a month—just before Georgia does her latest radio segment. Just like today, it might keep the crazies at bay.'

He blinked slowly. 'You said you didn't think it was a good idea to go out with me.'

She nodded. 'I'm not suggesting we date, just that once in a while we let ourselves be seen together in public, let everyone join the dots. It won't be our fault if they draw entirely the wrong picture.'

'And at work?'

'We do what we've been doing. Keep it cool and professional. People will think that we're trying to be discreet.'

He stared at her for the longest time. Chloe held her breath and refused to fidget. No way was she going to let him see how nervous she felt. She was very glad she let go of his hands now, because her palms were sweating.

It's not real. You're not asking him out on a real date...

'Why are you doing this for me?' he asked warily.

She shook her head. She didn't know, really. It was stupid. Crazy.

You do know, a little voice inside her head whispered. *You want an excuse to spend time alone with Drop-Dead Daniel, so you can make believe, torment yourself...*

No. That wasn't it. She couldn't *let* that be it.

'Someone told me about your sister,' she finally said. That was true. 'Let's just say I thought you could do with a break.' That was also true. It just hadn't been in her head when she'd put her proposition to Daniel.

His lips pressed together. 'I don't need your pity,' he said coldly, and he pushed himself up from the railing and walked off down the gallery.

Chloe let out a huff of frustration and then trotted after him. Damn male pride...

'It's not pity,' she said crossly as she closed in on him. 'It's a friend helping a friend. That's all.'

He stopped, pivoted around to face her. 'Friends? That's all?'

She nodded, not trusting her mouth to toe the party line.

He looked beyond her, up to the vast curving glass and ironwork ceiling. Despite his knee-jerk temper, he seemed to be chewing it over.

'I do confess I'm not being completely altruistic,' she added, finally finding something sensible to say, something much more slick and smooth and *Chloe* to say. The sort of thing he'd come to expect from her—ambivalent, flirty, slightly mocking. 'After all, you'll be paying for dinner.' And then she smiled brightly at him, just to prove there was nothing to worry about, that he needn't be scared of her getting the wrong idea and joining the ranks of his stalkers.

Amusement warmed his previously stony expression. 'Oh, I am, am I?'

She nodded again. This time because her mouth wasn't working, not because she was scared it was about to take off on its own.

There was something about his manner that completely changed. One moment he had been closed off, cold, almost backing away from her. But now there was fire in his eyes and even though she'd swear he hadn't moved he seemed to be getting closer.

Suddenly her cheeks felt very hot. She looked up at him, almost leaning over her.

'D-Daniel? What are you doing?'

'If it's my money we're going to be spending, my life we're going to be messing around with, then I get to say what goes.'

Her chin bobbed up and down. She got that. Daniel had been completely blindsided by the morning's events. He felt out of control. This request was just about reclaiming lost ground, that was all. She could let him have that much.

But then Daniel stepped towards her, pressing his body up against hers, pinning her between him and the wooden rail at her waist. His hands clutched the rail either side of her, his strong, taut arms preventing escape, and Chloe realised just how *off* her calculation of the situation had been.

It wasn't lost ground he was about to claim, but her.

He paused for a moment, just as his lips were millimetres from her. Her pulse lurched and her breath came in uneven bursts.

And then he was kissing her, expertly wiping any protest away with his firm lips. Chloe clung to his shirt for support. The difference in their height meant she felt she was arching back over the railing, feeling as if she'd fall at any moment.

But even that fear was quickly erased by the sensations erupting through her body. Sweet heaven, this was better even than she'd imagined it would be. He knew just when to take, just when to tease... Just how to leave her breathless and dizzy, even without the use of his hands, which were still making sure she stayed right where he wanted her.

If Chloe had been able to string a coherent sentence together, she'd have been able to tell him it wasn't necessary. As much as her brain was screaming for her to run, her body had been waiting too long for this. It was going to enjoy it while it lasted.

And enjoy it she did. Pretty soon her hands were unclenching from Daniel's T-shirt, exploring his rather fine chest, reaching up to pull him closer so she could really lose herself in him. Suddenly, she was claiming him back. And, damn, if that didn't just turn him on more. He moved his hands to her waist and for a second she thought he was going to lift her up and sit her on the rail. She grabbed him tighter, hoping he'd remember where they were, just how far she could fall if he lost concentration and let go.

She could feel him starting to lift her, his hands tightening around her ribs. She stiffened, and her eyes flew open, just in time to see him cock an eyelid. He pulled away, a decidedly wicked smile on his face, looking far more pleased with himself than a man had a right to after just such a stunt.

Even though she was pressing into him rather than leaning back over the railing, she still clutched onto him. At least she did until another noise filtered through her consciousness. She turned her head, slightly dazed, to find a small group of people on the ground staring up at them. Some of them were wearing the distinctive blue polo shirts with Kew's embroidered logo.

Drat. She'd forgotten they'd moved out of the cover of their secluded little corner.

Smiling nervously, she lifted her hand and gave them a little wave. They responded with a round of applause and a couple of wolf whistles.

She turned back to Daniel, keeping her eyes on his chest, and carefully smoothed his T-shirt flat with her palms before gathering the courage to look up at him.

'I thought the plan was to keep it discreet,' she said shakily.

Daniel's grin became even broader. Damn the man for enjoying this!

'Plans change,' he said, not in the least bit repentant. And then he stepped away and made tracks to the spiral staircase, whistling as he went.

Chloe walked forwards and rested her forehead

against the misty glass on the other side of the gallery. Not only had she *not* kept her distance from Daniel Bradford, but she'd actually proposed spending more time with him. Alone. In what messed up universe did that idea make sense?

She pressed her fingertips to her lips. She'd never had much self-control where Daniel had been concerned, and now look where it had got her. She'd made herself a trap, and she had no idea how she was going to climb out of it.

He found her in the orchid nursery the next morning, working on a plant she'd been growing from a seed that had lost its label during a collections trip. They needed to confirm what species it was, but until the plant flowered it was impossible to know. This one was stubbornly refusing. But Chloe knew all about being stubborn, didn't she?

The slight hesitation in her movement told him she'd heard him coming, but she carried on with her work. Not ignoring him, just finishing what she was doing. Indifferent, almost.

When she was ready she put the pot down and cocked an eyebrow. 'Well, if it isn't Indiana. Here to pound your chest?'

Daniel grinned at her. The way he was feeling this morning, a little chest pounding wouldn't be amiss. 'Don't know what you mean.'

'That's what that kiss was about, right? Putting on a good show, some macho attempt to mark me as yours?' She shook her head. 'All those jungle plants you work with must have activated your dormant monkey brain.'

Ouch. He was used to her being witty; he just hadn't realised she could be so cutting with it. But he liked *cutting*. It was way better than polite and impervious.

'Pretty much,' he said, looking her up and down. Today she was the smartest and slickest he'd ever seen. The pencil skirt had made a reappearance, along with a dark pink top and the trademark red lips.

He was lying, though. He hadn't had a plan. Not of any shape or any kind. He'd kissed her because he'd wanted to, because she'd been driving him crazy for weeks and he hadn't been able *not* to.

Since Valentine's Day he'd been at the mercy of the situation not of his making and he hated that. And, while Chloe's idea had merit, it felt an awful lot like being rescued. He hated that more. If anyone was going to be doing the rescuing it was going to be him.

So when the urge to kiss her had hit, he'd gone with it, had taken back control in one swift and delicious move. He wasn't prepared to regret it. Not after the way she'd responded to him. That had been no play-acting for the audience below. She'd been right there with him, dragging him deeper.

Indifferent? Yeah, right.

Chloe Michaels might do a good job of painting it that way on the surface, but underneath she was as hungry for him as he was for her. She just didn't want to admit it. Daniel didn't really care why. Not now he knew it was *game on* again—and that he'd had the first victory.

'Well, I'm glad that you got whatever it was out of your system,' she said starchily and turned her attention back to her orchid.

He moved a little closer. 'No action replays?'

She pursed her lips and scowled at him. 'I know the London press thinks you're God's gift, Indiana, but I think it's gone to your head. You're starting to believe your own hype.'

Daniel just chuckled. He so wasn't. But Chloe was acting as if he were as sexually neutral as that plant she was tending. He had a point to prove.

'Fine,' she said. 'If you don't like my idea, we'll scrap the whole thing. Good luck with the next raincoat flasher, though.'

'I didn't say I was backing out.'

Far from it.

'Well, then. We keep it on my terms,' she said. 'Strictly platonic. No more stunts like the one in the Palm House yesterday.'

'What if *you* cave and end up kissing *me* senseless?'

She made a scoffing noise. 'Not going to happen.'

He shrugged. 'Whatever you say. But if you give me the signals, I'm not going to ignore them.'

She let out a dry laugh. 'You are so big-headed! And so wrong.'

He so wasn't. But this was what he'd been waiting for from her. This was all part of the fun, the push and pull of the chase, letting her think she was in charge, when actually he was reeling her in bit by bit. She'd change her tune soon enough.

'How about that little Italian restaurant for our next outing?' he said.

Chloe's expression reminded him of how his grand-mother used to look at him over the top of her glasses. Even that made him want to whistle again. Oh, he was going to have so much fun with her. She was going to be worth every bit of this torturous wait.

Because he'd realised what he'd told Alan at the pub was true. There was more than one way to hunt. Chloe obviously didn't respond to the more direct approach—that only sent her running—so he was going to have to be more clever, more subtle. Just like his plants, he was going to make himself so irresistible to her that *she* wouldn't be able to help herself.

He thought of the species of *Sarracenia* whose tall pitchers contained narcotic liquor, drugging the insects it captured so they didn't even consider escaping. Chloe would be like one of those happy little flies when he'd finished with her.

'No Italian,' she said. 'I don't think the grapevine needs any more convincing at present. Yesterday did the trick quite nicely.' She picked up the pot and examined the moisture level. 'When's Georgia's next on-air segment?'

'I think it's the first Tuesday of the month,' he said.

She put the pot down again. 'Well, call me in June, then.'

Daniel grinned at her attempt to dismiss him. He'd go, but only because it was part of a bigger plan. He couldn't help letting her know that, though. He walked over to her, leaned in close and opened his mouth to whisper in her ear. She snapped the small green cane she was holding in half and every muscle in her body went taut.

So *not* indifferent.

'Till June,' he whispered, letting his breath warm the

sensitive parts of the ear lobe, and he actually saw the moment she suppressed a shiver.

Two more dates and he'd have her eating out of his hand.

As May bled into June Chloe got more and more agitated. Stupid, stupid idea. What had she been thinking?

Well, obviously, she hadn't.

She'd resorted to her old way of doing things, reacting on impulse rather than taking a measured decision. It was just that kind of behaviour that had got her into trouble with Daniel Bradford all those years ago, the sort of thing New Chloe didn't do.

Thankfully, however stupid her plan was, however self-destructive, it actually looked as if it was working. There had been no more 'raincoat' incidents, and Daniel had reported a drop in interested female visitors. The plan had its downside too, though. After being so excited to get her dream job as Kew's Head Orchid Keeper, Chloe now found her working days tense and stressful. She went home every evening with a headache.

It wasn't that Daniel had repeated the kiss in the Palm House. He'd kept his distance, just as they planned. Physically. That didn't mean he'd left her alone.

When they passed each other at work—which was often—he'd give her a smile he reserved just for her. Warm, intense...inviting. Just the sort of special smile lovers shared. It was messing with her head, big time. And he knew it.

Then, in early June, just as she'd suggested, Daniel's phone call came. He wanted to come and pick her up at home, but she made an excuse about having to work late, so he came and collected her from her nursery at the allotted time instead.

They walked through the gardens together to the staff car park. Plenty of people noticed their exit. Chloe could almost hear the whispers as they passed, see the nods and winks behind their backs. It was almost a relief to slide into the passenger seat of his car and shut the world out again. Or it would have been, if the clunk of the door hadn't created another little universe. A universe where the atmosphere became so hot the atoms danced and shimmered. A universe where she and Daniel were the only occupants. She faced forward and stared blindly at the windscreen. 'Where are we going?'

He just put the car into gear and pulled away. 'Somewhere lively,' he said, and Chloe's insides unclenched a little.

That was just what she needed. Somewhere busy, bustling with people. Somewhere she wouldn't be left alone with him.

The car joined the rush-hour traffic through Kew and on into Chiswick. Chloe's mood brightened further. There were some lovely restaurants here. She scanned the high street as they drove down it, wondering which one he'd picked.

Thai? French? Lebanese?

But when they turned into a side street he didn't park, even though there were plenty of spaces. Instead he kept driving, turning this way and that until he stopped in a residential street. They were outside a smart brick house with a large bay window and a glossy black front door. He turned the engine off and got out, opened the door for her. Chloe stayed in her seat, clutching her handbag.

'We're here?' she asked. 'Where are we?'

Daniel did a little bow. 'My house.'

She swallowed. 'I thought you said we were going somewhere lively.'

Daniel just smiled. 'You haven't been inside yet.'

Run, something inside her shouted. *Get out of the car and run.*

It was probably her common sense making a last-ditch attempt to save her. She let it scream its frustration then sprint down the road without her.

He held out his hand and she took it, let him help her from the car. Then he ushered her up the garden path and she stood aside while he produced his keys from his pocket and opened the front door.

The minute he'd stepped into the hallway he was practically bowled over by two running bundles of energy. Chloe blinked. It took her a second to work out they were two small boys, one a slightly smaller version of the other, both with Daniel's grey-green eyes.

He had...? They were...?

But then they both started shouting, 'Uncle Dan! Uncle Dan!' and the penny dropped. But the minute that puzzle had been solved another one elbowed its way in. This was where Daniel took girls on a *date*?

He turned and gave her a rueful smile, a small boy hanging off each arm, and led the way down the hall and into a kitchen-diner in the back of the house, with a lounge area under a conservatory at the far end. A tall, slender woman was stirring something on the hob.

Same dark hair with a bit of a kink, same pale eyes. That had to be his sister.

'Boys,' she said, 'try not to pull your uncle's arms off.' Then she looked up and smiled at Chloe. 'Hi.'

'Hi,' Chloe said.

'Welcome to the madhouse,' she said. 'I'm Kelly.' She indicated each of the boys in turn with her wooden spoon. 'That's Cal... That's Ben. Say hello to Uncle Dan's friend, boys.'

But the boys were too busy wrestling their uncle to the ground. For two people so small, they really knew what they were doing, Chloe thought, as Daniel's knees buckled and he was felled with a thud.

'They'll calm down in a minute,' Kelly said. 'They do that every night when he comes in.' She sighed. 'Their father took a hike a couple of years ago and the lack of male influence makes them a little full on when they get the chance to do some "boy bonding".'

Chloe's eyebrows rose. 'Beating each other half to death is *boy bonding*?'

Kelly grinned as she added some chopped tomatoes to the pan. 'You don't have brothers, do you?'

Chloe shook her head. Just her. And her doting, but rather hard to impress parents. It took a lot to carry the weight of all that parental expectation on one pair of shoulders. She'd often wished she'd had a sibling or two to share the load. 'Why can't they just paint each other's nails and snivel their way through a good film, like normal people do?'

Kelly laughed. 'Wow, it's good to have a bit of sanity around here. I thought I was in danger of drowning in all the testosterone. This house has been a bit lacking in female company since Georgia—' She bit her lip. 'Sorry.'

Chloe held up her hands. 'No, it's okay. Me and Daniel, we're just...'

Friends sounded so lame. *In cahoots* too much like a cheesy thriller. She settled for the safest option.

'...colleagues.'

Kelly scrubbed the pan with the wooden spoon. Chloe thought she could see a bit of burnt onion refusing to behave. 'Yep,' she said, giving the mixture a vigorous stir that made Chloe realise that Daniel wasn't the only one in the family who liked to get physical, 'and I'm just Gordon Ramsay.'

Chloe didn't say much after that. From the past couple of months at work, she knew it was no good to convince her otherwise. And it was an easy enough assumption to make. Why would Daniel be bringing her home otherwise?

The ruckus from the lounge end of the room was getting rather loud. Kelly handed the saucepan to Chloe and went to intervene.

'Boys!' she yelled. 'Pyjamas! Now!'

Instantly, the knot of testosterone on the floor disentangled itself. Then, one by one, they headed towards the stairs, pouts pushing their bottom lips forward. Daniel brought up the rear, copying their expression, which only made them giggle again. The whole scene would have descended back into chaos if Kelly hadn't given her big brother a clip round the ear.

The boys bounced in the doorway. 'We want Uncle Dan to read us a story,' they yelled repeatedly.

Uncle Dan looked up at Chloe, who was still holding the saucepan, and gave her an apologetic look. 'Do you mind?'

She shook her head. She'd been trying to keep her distance from him for weeks now. Why would she mind if he volunteered to do just that?

Kelly came and took the saucepan from her. Just as well Chloe had heard the thunder of little—and big—feet on the stairs, because Kelly's verdict on her own cooking was not for children's ears. 'I always was crap at cooking,' she explained. 'Dan said I should just get some posh stuff to reheat from the supermarket, but I had to decide to go all cordon bleu, didn't I?' She tipped the contents of the saucepan into the bin and banged it back down on the hob. Chloe quickly leaned forward and turned the gas off before another catastrophe occurred.

Kelly rummaged in a drawer and produced a fan of takeaway leaflets. 'Curry, curry, Chinese or curry,' she said brightly.

Chloe looked at the other ingredients lined up on the counter. Bacon, garlic, chilli flakes... 'Amatriciana sauce, right?'

Kelly nodded, looking at Chloe as if she were the bearer of ancient and hallowed wisdom.

'It'd be a shame to waste all that lovely fresh pasta,' Chloe said. 'Have you got another onion and more to-matoes? I'm sure I could help...if you wouldn't mind?'

Kelly looked as if she was going to prostrate herself at Chloe's feet. She grabbed Chloe's hand. 'Please marry him,' she said, and then she added, 'As you can see, my tact is as well developed as my culinary skills. Blame it on having two thickheaded brothers. Blunt and direct was what was required round our house when we were growing up. Never quite learned how to switch it off.'

Chloe grinned at her. She couldn't help liking Kelly. Her say-whatever-fell-into-her-head approach was rather refreshing. There must be something lovely about going through life like that, not having to worry about saying the wrong thing or accidentally showing a part of yourself you'd rather other people didn't know about.

'I take it there is wine somewhere in this kitchen?' she asked.

'Do you need it for the sauce?'

'No,' said Chloe, smiling. 'I need it in a glass. Now where are those tomatoes?'

Kelly provided both wine and tomatoes. 'Forget marrying Dan,' she said as she watched Chloe sweat some finely diced onion. 'Move in and adopt *me*.'

Chloe chuckled, and they continued to chat as she made headway in making the pasta sauce. Kelly was more a hindrance than a help, though, and Chloe quickly suggested she put her feet up, saying that looking after pre-schoolers must be very tiring.

She nodded in the direction of the ceiling as Kelly collected her wine glass and flopped on the sofa. 'He's great with the boys.'

'He is that.' Kelly looked up, a soft smile on her face. 'He'll make a really good dad some—' She froze, scratched her nose and looked away. 'Forget I said that.'

Inside Chloe was frowning, but on the outside she batted Kelly's stray comment away and smiled cheerfully back, mentally searching for something to say that would dispel the odd, slightly sad atmosphere that had settled on the other woman.

'Well, there is one thing I can guarantee,' Chloe said jokingly as she added some garlic to the pan. 'It's that I won't ever be marrying your brother.'

SIX

———

Daniel paused on the stairs as he heard Chloe's voice and smiled.

No marrying him. Ever. That was practically a guarantee.

He bounced back into the kitchen to find Chloe standing at the stove and Kelly lounging on the sofa sipping Merlot. What was wrong with that picture?

'I invited you for dinner,' he told Chloe, 'not the other way round.'

Chloe shrugged. 'I like cooking, and your sister...'

'Your sister burnt the crap out of the first attempt,' Kelly said helpfully. 'I've been banished to the sofa. She won't even let me help.'

Daniel gave his sister a very *brotherly* kind of look. 'And I can see it's just eating you up inside.'

Kelly held up her wine glass and toasted him with it before downing the remainder in one gulp. He shook his head and turned his attention to his guest.

'That smells amazing,' he said. 'You must be pretty good at this.'

She bowed her head and looked at the wooden spoon as she stirred the sauce. 'I like picking up new skills, perfecting them.'

Daniel smiled to himself as he and Kelly laid the table. His plan was working. He could tell from the way Chloe hummed to herself as she put the finishing touches to the pasta sauce that she was starting to relax. Just what he wanted.

He didn't want a date with starchy, let's-pretend-we're-being-discreet-at-work Chloe. He wanted a date with the Chloe who'd been within a hair's breadth of ripping his T-shirt off on the balcony of the Palm House. There was a girl who knew how to have fun.

He'd been given the job of cooking the pasta and she started teasing him when she realised it was overcooked and sticking to the bottom of the pan.

'Honestly,' she said, snatching it from him. 'The pair of you are as bad as each other. I don't know how those two poor children haven't starved to death.'

'I have extensive skills with a can opener and advanced microwave training,' he told her, quite seriously.

Kelly, who was now sitting at the table, glass of wine in hand, also piped up. 'And I make a mean chicken nuggets and oven chips.'

Chloe just shook her head.

'I'll bet you know how to make fancy pastry and everything,' Kelly said mournfully as they dished up.

Chloe tried to act nonchalant, but he could see just a hint of self-satisfaction in her reply. 'I've done a cookery course or two,' she said quietly.

His sister slumped on the table. 'Ugh. I hate women

like you,' she said dramatically, but the delivery just made Chloe laugh.

Daniel decided he was a genius. Kelly was probably his best weapon this evening. Chloe liked her, despite the fact that, beside his immaculately dressed and perfectly contained date, his sister seemed a little too loud and uncensored. It was like putting an elegant pink orchid and a dandelion in the same pot together: it shouldn't work. But the two women were getting on like a house on fire and he wasn't going to do anything to upset that.

Chloe *was* like one of her orchids, he decided as they chatted over the simple dinner. Beautiful. Poised. Aloof. Just like the graceful flowers she tended, she was almost too perfect to be true.

After dinner he moved to phase two of the plan. Kelly loaded the dishwasher, batting Chloe's efforts to help away and telling her she'd better leave it to the expert. Daniel made the coffee. Fresh not instant. One thing in the kitchen he could do really well. Then Kelly put her coat on and picked up her handbag.

Chloe's easy demeanour slipped a little. 'You're going?'

Kelly nodded. 'Big brother here promised he'd babysit tonight. He owes me.' She gave Daniel a knowing look. 'First night out with the girls in weeks,' she said, then she blew them both a kiss and hurried out of the front door before anyone could stop her.

Daniel brought Chloe a coffee and sat down at the table with her. He glanced at the comfy sofa in the conservatory, with ample room for two. That would have been his preferred location, but he sensed he needed to tread carefully now his secret weapon was off to the wine bar to drink cocktails with her girlfriends.

'For a long time Kelly wouldn't go anywhere,' he told Chloe. 'Too tired. Too self-conscious about her hair. It was very patchy when it first grew back.'

A look of pain crossed Chloe's features and she absent-mindedly fiddled with the end of a loose ringlet. 'How awful for her. Girls need their hair.'

He nodded, understanding that now. Personally, he wouldn't have cared if his hair was down to his knees or in a marine buzz cut, but the wallop Kelly had given him when he'd suggested, very practically, that she should just borrow his clippers and even it all out had let him know just how differently men and women saw this issue.

He and Chloe chatted about easy things. Safe things. Work. Plants. Mutual acquaintances. When she drained her cup, Daniel stood up and reached for the wine bottle. 'Another glass?'

She looked at him thoughtfully, and then she said, 'Just half. It was rather drinkable.'

He got fresh glasses from the cupboard as, thanks to Kelly's post-dinner clearing frenzy, the previous ones were already sloshing around in the dishwasher. But instead of joining her at the table he walked over and placed her glass on the table beside the sofa and then sprawled at the other end.

Chloe looked at him for a second and then stood up and came to join him, sitting neatly and very upright in the opposite corner. 'No funny business,' she said, and sipped her wine. 'You promised.'

He just smiled at her. 'I don't think I actually promised, but I did say that it would be up to you to make the first move.'

Chloe's shoulders relaxed a little, but her expression remained pinched. 'As nice as dinner was, I don't see how hiding away in your house is going to help us.'

'Ah,' he said. 'Well, it came about partly because I'd forgotten I'd told Kelly I'd babysit...' He frowned. 'In fact, sometimes I think she just pulls that one when she wants a night out, because I don't remember the original request at all.'

Chloe chuckled, and he knew he was taking the right approach. 'But then I realised it could help.'

Her eyebrows lifted.

'Kelly works in the admin office,' he told her.

'Oh, I didn't know that.'

'News that you've been round for dinner will be all around Kew—and I mean the district, not just the gardens—by noon tomorrow.

'The opening came up a couple of months ago. I saw the notice and suggested she apply. She needed something part-time—something that would fit around the boys and would help build confidence. And, as she told me quite pointedly, to stop her going insane after what seemed like months of being stuck indoors.'

Chloe had been clutching her wine glass against her chest and now she lowered it as she stared out of the windows at the darkening sky. 'She's very brave, isn't she?'

Daniel stopped looking at Chloe, stopped gauging every action and reaction, and joined her in staring out of the window. 'She says she's had to be. Wasn't her choice.'

He knew all about that. Knew all about surviving, not because he was strong and courageous, but because he was still alive and breathing, had found himself trudging onward with no choice about where to put his foot next. Sometimes survival wasn't a choice but a sentence.

But he didn't want to think about those dark days in his life. He wanted fun. He wanted to remember the joy in living.

A waft of Chloe's floral perfume hit him, dragging him back into the present, filling his nostrils and making his pulse kick. He turned to look at her. *This* was what was important. Now. This night, this woman. What he wanted right now was Chloe Michaels.

He caught her gaze, leaned in closer...

But she wasn't going to let him off the hook that easily. 'I haven't got any brothers or sisters,' she said, just the faintest twinge of envy in her voice.

Her parents must have thought they'd won the lottery, then, Daniel thought as he let his eyes rove over her once again. She was beautiful, confident, clever. She'd been their only chance and they'd lucked out. While other people...

Sometimes their only chance was wiped out before it had hardly begun.

He looked away and downed a huge mouthful of wine.

No. He'd shut that door. Done his grieving. He really wasn't going to think about it tonight. That would really be a buzz kill. He needed to get control of himself, of his thoughts.

But Chloe made it very difficult. He'd start on the track of conversation that seemed totally innocent, trying to get her to let down those polished walls a little more, and somehow he'd end up telling her things he didn't normally reveal to anybody—like the fact he had a touch of dyslexia, leading to stories about ridiculous errors with Latin plant names during his student days, something that only another horticulturist would truly appreciate. Or how he'd once accidentally leaned against a macaw palm during an expedition and had been picking its thorny black spines out of his backside for a week.

Talking to her was easy. As it had been with Georgia.

A chill rippled through him.

No. Chloe was nothing like his ex. He needed to remember that. This one was smart and savvy and she knew the game. Georgia...hadn't. But then he hadn't been playing games with Georgia. As cruel as it sounded, he'd just been passing time. And so had Georgia, she'd just tried to tell herself there was more to it.

But what was he doing thinking about his *almost* fiancée? He was losing focus. He'd invited Chloe here tonight with one thing in mind: to move forwards in his plan, and while she was relaxed and smiling he should press on.

He put his wine glass down and went to fetch the bottle from the kitchen counter. He filled his glass first then reclaimed his spot on the sofa, a little closer to Chloe this time, and he leaned across to top her up. She trailed off, losing the thread of what she was talking about, and her eyes widened as the wine filled her glass.

He placed the empty bottle on the table behind her head, but didn't move back. Their faces were only a couple of inches apart now. Unconsciously, she moistened her lips with her tongue, still staring at him.

He let go of the bottle and placed his hand on her

shoulder, curling his fingers round her nape. She shivered slightly as his thumb brushed her neck and her gaze dropped to his lips. His core temperature rose.

He slid the glass from her fingers and put it next to the empty bottle. She let him.

He didn't lean in and close the distance, though. Even though the air seemed to shimmer and thud between them. He'd told her the next move would be hers and he was going to stand by his word.

Okay, he hadn't left it completely up to her. He'd made a hundred little moves to manoeuvre her to this point, but the final leap would be all hers. There'd be no backing out then. No more running away and pretending she wasn't interested.

He heard, and felt, the shaky in-breath that parted her lips, watched her eyelids start to slide closed. He closed his eyes too, not wanting to distract himself in the sweet surrender he knew was coming...

There was a crash from the other side of the room, followed by a rhythmic thudding.

'Uncle Daniel!'

He opened his eyes to find Cal standing almost as close to him as he was to Chloe, looking between the two of them with open curiosity.

Chloe pressed herself backwards into the corner of the sofa and looked away.

'There's a crocodile under my bed,' Cal said, quite matter-of-factly. 'He wants to eat my toes.'

'Cal...' Daniel warned, his voice a little sharper than he'd intended it to be.

'He says he's going to gobble me up, bit by bit.' Cal

blinked, the picture of childish innocence. Had Kelly put him up to this?

Daniel was still so close to Chloe that he could feel her chest shaking as she tried to suppress a laugh.

Unfortunately, he wasn't finding this the least bit funny. He'd had his own plans for this evening. Maybe of a similar pattern—starting with the toes, and working his way up, bit by bit...

Just that thought alone made him ache.

Reluctantly, he got up off the sofa and took Cal back upstairs. A complete search—involving torches—was made of the under bed area, and it was only when Daniel had tucked the duvet in round his nephew and read him yet another story that Cal consented to lie down and close his eyes.

When he got back downstairs Chloe wasn't on the sofa where he'd left her, but in the hallway, putting on her coat.

'Thanks for a lovely evening,' she said. The dazzling smile she wore informed him that whatever barriers he'd managed to coax down in the last half-hour had sprung up again while he'd been hunting for Cal's crocodile.

Damn.

He couldn't wait another month to try again. It would seem like an eternity.

'Are you sure you don't want another glass of wine?'

Chloe shook her head and her curls bounced. 'I think I've had enough.' The seriousness that crept into her eyes told him she wasn't just talking about the Merlot. But he wasn't quite ready to let her go that easily.

'Think how much it would help our case if Kelly could tell everybody that you'd stayed for breakfast?'

Chloe sighed. 'Daniel… That's not the deal, and you know it.'

Damn again. So close.

'Maybe,' he said, smiling slowly. 'But optimism is one of my most appealing traits.'

At least she laughed. 'Of course it is,' she said and patted him on the arm as if he were an elderly aunt. Ouch.

He wanted to ask her to stay, to give him another chance, but it sounded suspiciously like begging inside his head, and he didn't do begging. Persuading, yes. Pursuing, definitely. But never begging.

The muffled hoot of a car horn outside took him by surprise.

'That's my cab,' she said.

Her cab.

She'd called a cab?

Suddenly Daniel didn't feel as firmly in control as he had been before. He liked the chase, but this quarry was intent on running him in new and unexpected directions. He couldn't quite decide whether he loved it or hated it.

'Night, Daniel,' she murmured, and then, without a flicker of hesitation or nerves, she leaned in close and pressed her lips gently to his cheek.

And then she was gone into the balmy night air, her little handbag swinging off her fingers.

Daniel shut the door when the cab drove away and gave out a loud growl of frustration.

'Uncle Daniel!' The terrified shriek came from Cal's room, and a few seconds later he was standing at the top of the stairs. 'The crocodile's back!' he said between sobs. 'And he's really, really angry.'

Daniel rubbed a hand through his hair and tramped up the stairs, scooping up the small, snivelling boy when he got to the top.

'Don't want to sleep in my room,' Cal hiccuped as Daniel headed across the landing. 'Can't I sleep with you?'

Daniel looked at the clock. Not even nine-thirty. When he'd dreamed of an early night, snuggling up with a warm body in his bed this evening, this was *not* what he'd had in mind.

He took his nephew into his darkened bedroom, making sure the landing light was on and the door wide, and he climbed on top of the covers while Cal slid underneath. It wasn't ten minutes before he could hear small-boy snoring and the rhythmic smack of Cal's lips against his stubby thumb.

Daniel lay there a little longer, just to make sure he didn't wake his nephew when he carried him back to bed. He couldn't be cross, not really. Both boys had been very clingy since their dad had left and Kelly had slipped into the habit of letting them sneak into her bed if they woke in the night.

As he lay there he stared at the wedge of orange light the street lamp had painted on his ceiling and let out a heavy breath. Chloe Michaels was a mystery to him. One minute she was all wide-eyed and trembling at his proximity, the next she was cool and detached and contained.

As much as he hated all those silly women turning up since George's proposal, at least they proved something—that he wasn't totally repellent. Quite the opposite. So why could Chloe resist him so easily? What made her so different? He just had to find out.

* * *

Thank goodness for small boys with crocodiles under their beds.

Chloe repeated the phrase to herself a hundred times as she got ready for work the next day.

Normally, she brushed her teeth on automatic, mind drifting, but this morning she watched herself in the mirror, her face free of make-up and her hair hidden beneath a twisted towel. She looked quite different from the woman who'd walked in the door last night.

She'd thought the Mouse was long gone, buried beneath years of being so cool and confident that play-acting had become reality. But she was still there. As Chloe brushed her teeth she occasionally caught a glimpse of her—something about a tightness in her jaw, a flicker of hesitancy in those eyes.

Chloe—the real Chloe—was glad she'd been handed an excuse to leave Daniel the night before. But the Mouse, stupid thing, was feeling all fluttery and excited about the way he'd looked at her, obvious desire in his eyes.

He wasn't looking at you, Chloe told the Mouse in the mirror. *He was looking at me. He likes me.*

The Mouse got all defiant then, asking her why, if Drop-Dead Daniel liked her, she wasn't doing anything about it. It was safe, after all, if the Mouse was really still safely under lock and key.

Why are you so scared...?

Chloe spat out her toothpaste and rinsed her mouth, and then she met her own eyes in the mirror again.

I'm not scared. It's just a bad idea.

Because...?

We are colleagues. We're... I just...

She pulled the towel from her head and released the damp curls darkened by the recent washing.

Okay, she admitted it. She was worried. Not scared, just a little concerned.

Because, as drop dead as he was, there was something about Daniel Bradford that burrowed beneath her armour.

Maybe it was because she'd liked him before New Chloe had taken form, because she had the oddest feeling he was the one person who had the power to crack her open and release the Mouse. Already the damn creature had come scratching around, making her say stupid things, do stupid things—like not breezily and smoothly disentangling herself when he first pressed his lips to hers in the Palm House. Like saying yes to that second glass of wine instead of going home.

She sighed. The Mouse wanted to relive that memory for a while, but Chloe shut it down swiftly.

No. It couldn't happen. She wouldn't let it. Because she couldn't go back to being that pathetic person. It would be too sad.

So she faced herself down in the mirror again, applied camouflage in the form of foundation and concealer, obliterated the creature with a wave of a magic mascara wand and her favourite tube of Valentine Rose lipstick. And when she was finished, she slid her feet into the highest, most impractical shoes she owned and made the journey to work.

SEVEN

———

Chloe found Daniel waiting for her outside the tropical plant nurseries after work. A large wicker picnic basket was swinging from his hand. She stared at it, already guessing where they were going for their July date. Just as well she'd changed into something casual and summery.

'I hope you like live music,' he said.

She nodded and smiled, determined not to show she was nervous at the prospect of another evening in his company.

While all months at Kew had their own special appeal, July was bold and bright and showy. Everywhere flowers bloomed, filling the gardens with a stunning palette of colours and a cocktail of scents. They walked the half-mile to their destination: past the Palm House, through the Mediterranean garden with its temple, and on to the largest of Kew's glasshouses, the Temperate House.

Each year Kew hosted a week-long music festival, erecting a stage in front of the three-sectioned greenhouse. As dusk fell the Temperate House became the backdrop for the performance, and coloured lights inside would bathe the trees emerald and turquoise and magenta, and bands would play into the night as the audience picnicked on the lawn in front.

The music selection was different each night. There was classical. There was jazz. There were top-name chart acts and old-timers touring on a second wind of fame. Tonight, Kat de Souza, one of the rising stars of the UK music industry, was playing.

Chloe had asked Emma if she wanted to come, but she'd cried off, saying some hot young guy had turned up at her belly-dancing class a couple of weeks ago and she didn't want to miss one in case he came back. So, secretly, Chloe was very pleased Daniel had chosen this for their July 'date'.

He led her to a reserved section of lawn near the stage, pulled a thick woollen blanket from the top of the basket and spread it on the ground. Chloe sat down as elegantly as she could in her knee-length summer dress, crossing one leg over the other. He wrestled with something in the picnic basket behind her and then there was the distinctive breathy pop of a champagne bottle being opened. Seconds later he passed a slim flute to her.

'Thank you,' she said and took a sip. 'This is lovely, if a bit...well...public.'

He sat down beside her and lounged back, stretching his long legs out and resting on one elbow. 'You complained our last date wasn't public enough.'

'I did not complain. I merely commented,' she said in her smoothest voice.

Daniel chuckled. 'Believe me, after living with my

sister for the last year and a half, I am well aware that in the female species those terms are practically interchangeable.'

'Rubbish,' Chloe said, but her lips curled at the edges.

He just raised his eyebrows and did a pretty passable impression of Kelly. 'Daniel, there are muddy boots in the hallway... Daniel, there's some weird compost—like rotting muesli—in the bathroom sink...'

Chloe couldn't help but laugh. She liked this side of Daniel. When she'd first come back to Kew she'd thought him more buttoned-down than before. But he seemed much more like his old self now. Maybe it had just been a result of all the stressful press attention in those early months.

He unpacked the picnic—one of Kew's gourmet affairs that he must have pre-ordered when he'd booked the tickets. Just as well, given Daniel's culinary skills. There were appetisers and Greek salad, poached salmon and strawberries and cream. Chloe helped herself to a miniature tartlet. It was heavenly.

The last month had gone seamlessly. The Mouse had been banished and she and Daniel were executing their plan perfectly. They'd reached a silent understanding after their last date. As a result, it wasn't awkward when they bumped into each other at work any more. He often dropped by her nursery when he was passing, occasionally bringing her a cup of her favourite coffee from the nearby café. They were friends. And if people saw their easy banter and read more into it, then she let them.

The first act came on as the sun fell low in the sky and music permeated the balmy evening air. Chloe leaned back on her hands and felt all the tension melt from her shoulders.

They were good. A lively little swing band that had the audience's toes tapping and heads nodding. She and Daniel worked their way through the picnic and a little more of the champagne. He was attentive, giving her the lion's share of the strawberries, offering to top up her glass if it got too low, and they chatted easily as the band played and twilight fell.

And he was being the perfect gentleman, which made things so much easier.

Chloe sighed with contentment. So she didn't want to get romantically entangled with Daniel. It wasn't a crime to spend time with a man who enjoyed being with her. And he *did* enjoy being with her. She could tell that from every look, every scrap of body language.

She should have paid attention to the wave of warmth that flooded her torso at that thought, but she didn't. She was too busy stripping the ghosts of the past of all their power.

Before, she'd just been a faceless girl to him. One of the many anonymous bodies in a packed lecture hall. He hadn't known her when he'd pushed her away, told her to get a grip on herself. But now...

Now Daniel did know her, and he liked what he saw. It changed everything.

So when the breeze picked up and Chloe gave a little shiver, causing Daniel to shift closer so she could rest against his shoulder if she wanted to, she didn't wriggle away. And when the swing band finished their set and everyone got up to dance for their final number, she let him pull her to her feet.

The music was so loud that he had to lean in very close to talk into her ear. His breath was warm on her neck. 'You're good at this,' he said, after she spun out and then back in again. 'You've got the moves right down.'

Chloe showed off by doing a tuck and spin. 'I had a few lessons,' she said, a little smugly.

Daniel looked suitably impressed. He twirled her out again perfectly, but when she came back he was closer and she all but crashed into him. Her palm splayed across his chest was the only thing that stopped the entire length of their torsos touching.

'You're a woman of many talents,' he said, sliding his hands round her waist. 'Are you this good at everything you do?'

'I make sure I am,' she replied. She'd meant it quite innocently, but the husky tone to her voice added a whole extra layer of meaning.

Daniel's eyebrows rose in reply and his smile widened. Then he pulled her closer so her temple was pressed against his cheek. 'I'll bet you are,' he whispered into her ear, and Chloe started to shake deep down inside.

The song came to an end and people started clapping. Chloe and Daniel didn't move. An invisible force field had glued them together, even when the applause faded and people started sitting back down to continue eating and drinking in the break before the next artist. The slap of the double bass was still pounding in Chloe's ears, even though the band had left the stage minutes ago.

There was no comfortable, easy conversation now.

They'd gone beyond words, the delicious little undercurrent zapping between them was doing all the talking.

Would it really be so bad?

To give in to this tugging deep down inside, the one that was drawing her to Daniel? They were both single, both grown-ups. Wasn't this what she'd wanted—longed for—for years? She couldn't quite remember why she was so set on denying herself now.

While she was still contemplating this, the stage darkened and the crowd hushed in anticipation. Reluctantly, they pulled apart and sat down as Kat de Souza walked onto the stage, her feet bare, in tight fitting jeans, a simple sleeveless black T-shirt and a multitude of necklaces and bangles. When she reached the centre she sat down on a stool. Everyone went quiet. Chloe could even imagine the trees in the arboretum leaning just a little bit closer to listen.

Kat's first song was one of her early hits. Chloe found herself mouthing the words and swaying slightly, knees bent, feet together, body hugged against her knees. She was completely lost in the moment until she heard a deep, rich voice beside her, humming. She turned to find Daniel singing.

She leaned closer so he could hear her without her shouting. 'You know every note.'

He gave a rueful smile. 'Kelly mainlined this album for about three months. I could probably recite the lyrics in my sleep, if I really wanted to. It's not really my kind of stuff, but it grew on me.'

'Let me guess,' Chloe said. 'You're more of a rock guy?'

He smiled at her in a way that made her insides avalanche. She turned to face the stage again and carried on singing silently, feeling a wee bit oxygen starved.

The song was a bewitching one of love and passion and regret, and the magic it wove throughout the crowd deepened the spell working on Chloe. The sky grew dark, the rainbow lights in the Temperate House glowed and the champagne danced in her veins. Daniel shuffled in behind her and she sank back into him, while she kept her eyes on the young woman on the stage.

Every part of her that touched him was fizzing with electricity, and she didn't want it to stop. And that only meant one thing.

Dared she really do this? Was she really that brave?

Daniel moved so he could talk into her ear. 'Your lips are moving, but you're not making any sound.'

She twisted towards him and found his face breathtakingly close. 'How do you know? I was facing away from you and it's too loud to hear me even if I was.'

His arm snaked around her and he flattened his palm against her lower ribs. And then he just looked at her. Looked into her eyes. Looked at her lips. 'I can't feel any vibrations in your torso,' he said quietly.

He couldn't? Chloe sure as hell could.

But he was right—she hadn't been singing.

'Singing is the one thing I've never been any good at, no matter how hard I tried.' And, boy, had she tried. Two years of private singing lessons hadn't been able to get a good note out of her.

Strangely, this made Daniel smile.

'What?' she said, knowing her cheeks were colouring further.

'It's nice to know you've got a few imperfections like the rest of us.'

He'd meant it as a compliment, but Chloe couldn't help the instinctive bristling at his words. A spike of something cold went through her. She was an attractive, confident, sexy woman now. It had been a long time since her parents' suffocating ambition for her had weighed on her heavily. She knew she didn't have to be brilliant at everything, but it was hard to let go of the little inner push that told her to try harder, be better. And she was feeling a little of that pressure tonight.

New Chloe had been her most important self-improvement package to date. What was the point in excelling at Italian cooking or swing dancing or Spanish guitar if you failed at the most important thing—being a woman? Deep down inside, even if she hadn't admitted it to herself, her decade-long quest had been to turn herself into the kind of woman Daniel Bradford wouldn't turn down. And tonight, if she was brave enough, she could have her answer. One way or another.

Oh, the thought scared her so. She went to turn her head away, catch her breath for a moment, but he caught it with his hand, hooking his fingers round the curve of her neck, letting his thumb trail her cheek. 'Don't.'

She held her breath.

This was it, wasn't it? She could reach for what she wanted—what she'd always wanted—or she could shrink back like a coward.

She took in every feature of his face, lingering over the line of his jaw, the not quite straight nose, the tiny scar she'd never noticed before almost completely hidden by his left eyebrow.

And he held still and let her, meeting her gaze. Not flinching, as she might well have done.

This wasn't the same as that awful night in the pub car park ten years ago. How could it be? He'd been giving her the signals for months. He wasn't going to push her away, this time. He wasn't going to run.

She swallowed and dropped her gaze to his lips, knew the exact moment he did the same.

Stop, a voice inside her head said. *You've been here before. You remember how it ends.* But even this voice sounded half-hearted and unconvincing.

Keeping her eyes fixed on the firm curve of his lower lip, she leant forward to taste it.

Daniel stayed completely still at first, letting her discover the hint of strawberries still lingering on his mouth. She took her time, exploring fully—the little dents at the corners of his lips, the fullness of the bottom one, the sculptured curve of the top.

And then something seemed to snap inside him and he hauled her onto his lap and took over. If Chloe had thought that sweet, slow exploration had been worth a decade of waiting, Daniel's fully-loaded response was more than she ever could have imagined. It swept conscious thought and common sense completely from her brain.

Daniel's head was spinning. Kissing Chloe was every bit as good as he remembered. Possibly better. Because this time she wasn't blindsided, taken by surprise. This time he'd let her come to him, let her take charge.

Why, for heaven's sake, had he never used this approach before? He'd still been hunting, but it hadn't been a crashing-through-the-forest kind of hunting; it had been patient and stealthy, all about the wait rather than the pursuit, and the prolonged anticipation had only made the final moment so much sweeter. Instead of feeling as if he'd worn her down, broken something inside her to let him in, he felt alive because she was blooming right there in his arms.

When they pulled away from each other, her eyes stayed closed, a delicious little smile on her lips. Daniel was very tempted just to lean in close and taste them again, but he wanted her to open her eyes and look at him.

She was a contradiction, this Chloe Michaels. He'd expected her to be as slick and expert with her lips as she was in everything else. She was, but not in the way he'd anticipated. There'd been a rawness, a sweetness, an exuberance to her response that had caught him totally by surprise.

Her lids parted and she held his gaze.

It was there. What he'd been waiting to see, even though he couldn't quite put a name to it.

Once wasn't enough. Not nearly enough. But he had to keep reminding himself he was sitting on a lawn with a couple of thousand other people, and that it might not be the greatest idea to keep going right now. He knew where he wanted to spend the night, and it wasn't in a police cell.

As good as the music was, it was torture to wait for Kat to finish her set. He kept in contact with Chloe any way he could. He wrapped himself around her, linking his arms in front, pressing butterfly kisses into her neck and hearing the low noises of appreciation deep in her throat as she closed her eyes and tilted her head to give him better access.

Eventually, the last chord was played, the applause welled and faded, and the stage lights dimmed. People around them began to move. Daniel reluctantly peeled himself away from Chloe and stood up.

'I'll be back in a second,' he told her and disappeared off to a marquee to dispose of the now-empty picnic basket and supplies.

When he returned, he saw her long before he cleared the rest of the crowd. She was the only thing in focus as he made his way towards her, the soft smile on her lips, the way her eyes took on extra sparkle when she looked at him... It was making his blood simmer.

He had to kiss her again when he reached her, couldn't help himself, couldn't get close enough.

'This time I'm taking you home,' he said, stepping away and turning in the direction of the car park.

She tugged him back and delayed him with another swift kiss. 'Not that way,' she murmured huskily. 'We can walk through the gardens and leave through the gate near the river. I only live a few minutes from there.'

Daniel thought of the modern apartment blocks on the other side of the river. Dark wood, white stucco and steel. They suited her perfectly. Stylish, modern, free from any clutter and complications.

They walked through the gardens in silence. Every now and then they paused to kiss—one moment with her pressed up against the rough bark of a tree, the next in the middle of a lonely path, beautiful vistas spreading out unseen around them in every direction. Each meeting of their bodies and lips grew more heated, more frantic. Daniel realised he needed to slow this down a little or he'd explode before they even reached the boundary of the park. As wonderful as making love to Chloe on the soft dark grass would be, if Security caught them they'd both be out of a job in the morning.

Finally they reached Brentford Gate and walked through the car park and along the tow path. The lights in the apartment blocks glinted temptingly across the water and he willed himself to last until they got there. However, it was only a few steps before Chloe stopped and turned.

'Here we are,' she said.

Daniel frowned and looked around. There were no houses here, just trees. Not even a path or a gate to a back garden, as there were farther up the tow path.

'No...this way,' she said softly and tugged at his hand. He turned one-eighty, but all he could see past the row of houseboats was the river, glinting gold and silver from the moon and the streetlights on the far bank.

Houseboats...

He stopped looking at the water and turned his attention back to Chloe. 'Here?'

'Come aboard,' she said, pulling his hand and heading down a narrow gangplank to a double-storey boat with a flat roof, decorated with enamel buckets full of summer flowers.

He was a little confused at first. This really wasn't the sort of place he'd pictured her living in. It was charming enough, but it wasn't slick and luxurious like Chloe herself. However, he quickly decided he didn't really care where she lived. That she was actively dragging him inside was the important thing, surely?

He followed her down into the cabin, and the interior was as much of a surprise as the outside. Half of the top deck was a living-dining-kitchen area with vast square windows one end that led onto a railed deck.

No clean lines and minimalist furniture here. It was a riot of colour and texture. Two purple velvet sofas that didn't match, embroidered and bejewelled cushions in pinks, reds and oranges. Bookcases lined one wall, full of not only gardening books and paperbacks, but all other kinds of ornaments. And, of course, there were orchids. Various common varieties, but also some spectacular rarer ones too.

Chloe walked over to the kitchen and kicked off her shoes. 'I'm afraid my drinks selection is rather sparse,' she confessed. 'Unless you're really gasping for mineral water, it's just white wine.'

He nodded. 'That'll do fine.'

He knew he should sound more enthused, but he couldn't quite stop looking around Chloe's living room. It wasn't just that every corner held something that drew the eye, but that he felt something about it was significant. Something he was missing.

He walked over to the kitchen and took a glass she offered. Without her shoes on she was just that little bit shorter, which, for some strange reason, also made her seem younger.

'I didn't picture you living on a houseboat,' he told her.

She smiled at him. 'I always wanted to, ever since I was a student here and used to walk past them on my journey from Kew Bridge station. When I got the chance to rent one, I jumped at it.'

He took a sip of his wine. 'Of course, I forgot you said you trained here. When was that? Our paths might have crossed. I've been doing specialist lectures here for what...maybe eight or nine years?'

Chloe suddenly found something very urgent to do in the fridge. She opened the door, blocking his view of her, and rummaged around inside.

Daniel smiled to himself. Possibly not. He'd certainly have remembered seeing someone like Chloe amongst the muddy hordes of horticultural students. She stood out in a crowd, wasn't like the rest. That was what he liked about her.

Anyway, he was much more interested in the here and now. Chloe was still leaning into the large retro-style fridge and he walked up behind her and slid his hands around her waist. Whatever she'd been looking for in there obviously hadn't been very important, be-cause she stood up, let the fridge door bang closed and turned to face him, her face serious, her pupils wide.

He dipped his head low and kissed her. Softly, slowly. This had been a long time coming and he didn't want to rush things. Strangely, it seemed as if he were kissing her for the first time. Maybe it was this place—or this slightly shy and nervous Chloe—that made him feel as if this were all fresh and new.

Whatever it was, he decided both of them were wear-ing far too many clothes, even though, including linge-rie, Chloe must have only had three garments on. Heat flooded through him. He didn't care which one went first—each presented an interesting option—but some-thing needed to go, and it needed to go now.

He'd never been one for noting clothes designers, but

he blessed the man, because it had almost certainly been a man, who'd decided to put a long row of little hooks and eyes down the front of Chloe's tight-bodiced floral dress. His fingers fairly itched at the thought of starting at the top and working his way down.

Maybe he was wrong about three garments. Maybe a little exploration in that department would yield even richer results. He'd been kissing her neck, hands roving her back, and now he moved on to either side of her waist, then he picked up and deposited her on the kitchen counter. She ran her hands up his chest and into his hair, pulling him back to kiss her on the mouth, pulling him closer and hooking her lower calves around his thighs to keep him there.

In Daniel's experience, some women let a man take charge completely when it came to the physical stuff but he much preferred it if there was equality, give and take, when they got to this moment. So he liked the fact that Chloe not only responded to him but spurred him on, took him in new and unexpected directions.

Even better, he could tell by the way she threw her head back and closed her eyes, the little noises she made in the back of her throat, the unchoreographed motions of her hands, that none of this was rehearsed moves or seductive tricks. She was totally lost in the moment, and this response that had his clothes feeling three sizes too small was just pure Chloe.

He pulled away from kissing her to focus his eyes on the top of her dress. The hooks were tiny. He could've undone them by touch alone, but he wanted to see her, every perfect inch, when he reached low enough to uncover what was underneath.

Chloe was kissing his face, and when she felt the pads of his thumbs graze the upper curve of her breasts as he reached for the first hook she made a sharp intake of breath and held it. Her legs hugged him tighter, pulling him as close as he could possibly get still clothed.

Daniel suddenly questioned the hook-by-hook approach. What idiot made something so small and fiddly? He was really tempted to just start ripping.

Chloe fidgeted again, but this time she placed her hands lightly on his chest. 'Daniel...' she whispered.

He leant in and began to tease her ear lobe with his tongue. 'Uh-huh?'

There was a little bit of a push behind those palms now. He drew back, confused. Were they both not on the same track? Had he read her wrong somehow?

But the pink flush creeping up her creamy skin from breasts to face told him he'd been reading the situation just right. 'Are you okay?' he asked softly.

'Oh, yes,' she said, nodding emphatically. 'More than okay.'

Daniel smiled. Not just because she was as into this as he was, but because he'd never seen this flustered, slightly dishevelled side to Chloe before, and he kind of liked it. Somehow it made her seem all the more human. Which translated into making her seem all the more touchable. His gaze drifted back to the single opened hook at the centre of her breasts.

'I just need to...' Chloe shakily pushed her hair back off her face and released her legs from around his. 'There's just something I need to do...I'll be right back.'

'Promise?' he said, feeling a lot more desperate than he actually sounded.

She smiled sweetly at him, and pressed a kiss against his lips. 'Promise,' she murmured as she pulled away.

She jumped down from the counter and picked up her shoes. 'I won't be long.'

He wandered over to the bookcase. His eyes instantly found a spine that was so familiar he couldn't help but prise it from its position. She turned as she reached the door and saw what he was doing.

She smiled saucily. 'Isn't that a little vain? Picking your own book out from the bookshelf?' Forgetting her urgent errand, she walked over to him. '*The Secrets of Mount Kinabalu* by Daniel Bedford,' she read from the cover. 'I got this as a student. Your description of the orchids is what fired my interest in them.'

He shook his head, both frowning and smiling at the same time. 'I can't believe you've got this,' he said. 'And it looks as if it's been read a hundred times.'

Chloe stiffened slightly but then she smiled her cat-like smile again. 'I lent it out to other people in my year. It was kind of a favourite.'

'That's a lot of people with a burning interest in carnivorous plants and other rare species,' he said.

Chloe just laughed, reached out and turned the book over, where there was a horrible picture of him in khaki clothes and a wide-brimmed hat. 'I think this is what some of them had the burning interest in,' she said. 'This is where the whole Indiana Jones thing started, wasn't it?'

He nodded grimly. He hadn't made the connection before, but he supposed it was. 'Some fool publicist's idea. I've always hated the stupid picture.'

'I'll bet you sold a load more books because of it, though. Didn't I hear talk of a TV series once?'

Daniel snorted. 'I knocked that one on the head pretty fast.'

She took the book from him and leafed through it, smiling as if she was remembering happy memories. She stopped at a colourful plate of a particularly rare slipper orchid. 'Did you really take this picture? See it yourself?'

He gave her a one-sided smile and nodded.

'I wish I could,' she said wistfully. 'I can't think of anything more beautiful.'

He reached for her face, brushed a golden tendril away from her cheek and slid his fingers into her hair before pulling her closer for a soft, sweet kiss. 'I've seen it for myself,' he whispered, 'but, believe me, it's nothing compared to what's in front of me right now.'

Chloe caught him by surprise. She threw her arms around his neck, gave him a hot, drawn-out kiss, promising all sorts of things that got him very excited indeed. And it hadn't even been a line. He really did think she was more stunning than the speckles and stripes of the elusive flower.

When she finally pulled away, she rested her forehead against his and breathed out hard.

'Didn't you say you...had something to do?' he said hoarsely.

She nodded wordlessly and he let his arms drop.

As much as he didn't want to let her go, he didn't want to interrupt things later on. Daniel didn't want to be distracted by anything next time he had Chloe in his arms. Not for hours and hours and hours.

EIGHT

———

Chloe ran quickly and lightly down the narrow hallway that led to her bedroom. Once inside she pulled the duvet straight and plumped a pillow, then turned her attention to the other item that needed to be dealt with: the graduation photo sitting on her bedside table.

Ugh. Frizzy hair and badly applied eyeshadow.

She only displayed it in the privacy of her bedroom because she was really, really proud of her qualifications, even if the tight smiles of her parents standing behind her reminded her how they'd have preferred for her to go to a big-hitting university and get a 'proper' degree.

She couldn't risk just putting it face down, so she pulled the underwear drawer of her dressing table open and stuffed the frame under the tangle of straps and things. But the sight of some of her better underwear sitting in the top of the drawer made her stop and think.

She hadn't been planning on anyone seeing her underwear when she'd got dressed this morning. It was nude-coloured and functional. Nice enough, just not pretty like those were.

And you're planning on someone seeing your underwear now?

Chloe thought for a moment.

Hell, yeah.

The problem was that her current bra was strapless and her dress had spaghetti straps. It would be weird if she changed into her eye-wateringly expensive silk and lace set and went out there with hot-pink straps showing. Not very subtle.

Forget subtle. Ditch the dress and go back out there in just the pink satin with the creamy lace trim.

Chloe let out a gasp. She couldn't, could she? She'd never been quite that bold before—at least, not on a first night together. It wasn't her.

Or was it?

The Chloe she'd invented for herself to grow into would do it. She was sassy and worldly-wise and confident. Maybe she never had before, but that was because she liked a man to do all the running, to *prove* he was interested. And, deep down, if she admitted it to herself, she liked it that way because then it was him not her who had to endure that horrible feeling of free fall once he'd made the first move and was waiting to see if she'd accept or reject him.

But this time it was different. The way Daniel had been looking at her...touching her... Well, she was pretty sure he wasn't going to try and fend her off this time.

Maybe she needed to do this. Not to get him to prove anything, but to prove something to herself.

Quickly, before she could talk herself out of it, she

stripped off her underwear and reached for the pink silk. Once it was on, she turned to inspect herself in the mirror.

There were a few lumps and bumps she wished weren't there. After prodding her stomach, which jiggled a little, she looked longingly at the functional bra and knickers and sundress on the floor. There was something about walking out there as she was now that made her feel very...naked.

She looked herself in the eye and pulled herself up straight, sucked things in a little. That was what New Chloe would do. So she had a few curves, but Daniel didn't seem to mind, and she wasn't that blobby little nineteen-year-old any more. New Chloe knew she worked out, that she was toned. New Chloe knew she looked good.

She bent down, picked up her discarded clothes and threw them in the wardrobe. A pair of hot-pink heels winked at her from inside and she quickly reached for them and slid them on her feet. Then, without looking back, she strutted down the corridor back to the living room, reminding herself to breathe.

Since Daniel had picked up a framed photo of her on holiday last year, she took the opportunity of reaching for the dimmer switch and taking the lighting down to a more *intimate* level as she entered the room.

The change in brightness made him look up and round to where she was standing.

He dropped the frame.

It bounced on the floor but didn't break.

The look on his face right then was all Chloe needed

to wipe all those years of insecurity away. Never had she felt so feminine, so beautiful...so wanted.

She could pull this off, she really could. New Chloe had been a project that had worked from the outside in, but she had the feeling that after tonight that version of herself would no longer be a work in progress. One night with Daniel Bradford would banish the Mouse for ever and cement New Chloe into place. The transformation would be complete.

Since Daniel didn't seem capable of movement at the moment, let alone speech, she walked slowly towards him, crouched to pick up the picture—aware that the angle of her knees and the high heels were doing amazing things for her legs—and handed it back to him and nodded towards the bookcase. He replaced it without taking his eyes off her.

And then, taking advantage of his paralysed state, which only gave her some kind of weird exultant power, she gave him a gentle shove and he sat down suddenly on the sofa. She had one knee on the sofa beside his leg, preparing to slide onto his lap, when he shifted slightly and reached beneath him. He pulled out the book—his book—that she'd thrown there earlier. Knowing they were definitely not going to be doing any reading in the next few hours, Chloe took it from his fingers and tossed it onto the adjacent sofa cushion.

As she did so a slip of coloured paper dislodged itself from the pages and fluttered to land on Daniel's lap. He picked it up and stared at it. Chloe took the opportunity to place her other knee on the sofa and sank down until soft, rounded bottom met hard thighs. She attempted to pluck the paper from his hands, but he wouldn't let go.

'What's this?' he asked, obviously having recovered the use of his tongue. Chloe wasn't very happy about that. For the money she'd paid for this bra and the way it made her boobs look he should have been drooling, his tongue thick in his mouth, for at least another half-hour.

He frowned. 'Who...? Why have you got this?'

It was then she realised it was a photograph.

'That's me,' he said, sounding slightly dazed, 'in the middle.'

Chloe's stomach rocketed down so hard she reckoned it had gone through the hull of her houseboat and was now wedged in the mud at the bottom of the river.

She'd forgotten all about that photo, tucked lovingly in the back of her favourite book, the one she'd never, *ever* lent to anyone else. A snap someone had taken on the last day of Daniel's tropical plants course of a bunch of students and their much-admired lecturer.

'Oh, that,' she said blithely, trying once again to dislodge it from his fingers without seeming as if she was desperate. 'That's from my college days.'

'You attended my course?' he asked, still looking at the photo and not the pink lingerie. That was starting to annoy Chloe.

She let out a huff of air. 'I told you I was a student at Kew,' she said.

Finally, he made eye contact. He still wasn't letting go of the photo, though. 'Why didn't you say anything?'

Chloe swallowed. What was she going to tell him? That she was the girl who'd humiliated herself in front of him? No way. 'When we first met it was obvious you didn't remember me—why would you?—so I decided not to bring it up. I didn't want to make you feel awkward.'

Hah! Biggest fib ever. It had been nothing to do with not wanting *Daniel* to feel awkward.

He frowned and looked back at the photograph. 'I do remember a few of these people,' he said slowly, his eyes flitting between one face and the next.

Chloe decided drastic measures were needed. In a few seconds he'd realise *she* was in that photo. And while he hadn't put two and two together yet, that didn't mean he wouldn't if he stared at it long enough.

She peeled his fingers from the photograph, let it flutter to the floor and placed his hands high on her waist, just on her lower ribs, and then she leaned forward and delivered the kiss of her life.

Thankfully, after a few seconds, she felt him relax, felt his jaw soften as he kissed her back. She let him set the pace, take control, knowing that was what he needed at that moment to keep his mind occupied. Within sixty seconds she wasn't thinking about anything but his lips and the lazy circles his thumbs were making on her torso, travelling slowly upward. If he didn't get to that pink silk soon she was going to explode.

Just as he'd pulled her closer, as his thumb had grazed the underside of her breast and Chloe had let out a low moan, his hands slowed down. And then they stopped. She tried to keep on kissing him but eventually his lips stopped too. He pulled away.

Chloe's heart raced, and not from the recent thumb activity. This time her pulse was struggling to push frozen blood through her veins.

He leaned past her to reach for the photograph at his

feet, and Chloe slowly climbed off his lap. He picked it up and looked first at the photo and back at her, then he studied the photo again.

When he spoke his words were measured and cool. 'Where are you in this photograph?'

Chloe shook her head, lips moving, not able to produce any sound.

Daniel's brows lowered. 'Don't lie to me,' he said. 'Don't tell me you're not in here.'

A tiny noise escaped her mouth. The kind of weak croak any self-respecting frog would be ashamed of.

The urge to curl up and hide was irresistible. She knelt on the other side of the sofa and buried her face in her hands, hiding her exposed flesh as much as possible.

Daniel leapt to his feet. 'All the time it was you and you never told me! What is this? Some kind of sick joke? You're...you're just like the rest of them...just another obsessive woman.'

The tears began to stream down Chloe's face. She wiped the first wave away and looked at him, still trying to curl into the sofa and disappear. 'That's not true! I made it quite clear from the beginning I didn't want to get involved, but you just kept wearing me down...'

He let out a harsh, dry laugh. The look on his face was pure revulsion. 'That was all part of the plan, wasn't it? And I fell for it—hook, line and sinker. That idea to "help" me out with those fake dates...' He shook his head, as if he was hardly able to believe the thoughts running through his head. 'God, I was suckered right in, wasn't I?'

Anger was taking over now, and Chloe let it. It was a much better sensation than cold humiliation. She stood up and folded her arms tightly across her chest. 'There was no plan! You're being paranoid.' She walked right up to him. He backed away.

That hurt.

'Admit it!' she yelled. 'You did all the chasing. You wouldn't leave me alone. That wasn't a trick. You *wanted* me!'

His expression set like stone. 'I wanted *her*,' he said softly, almost too reasonably. 'The woman I thought you were. Not—' he gestured towards the photo still in his right hand '—this.'

Chloe's ribs tightened so hard that she couldn't open her mouth to breathe.

'I would never want *this*,' he said, glaring at the photo and then transferring that scalding gaze to her. 'Not the sort of person who lies and manipulates, who can't just come out and tell the truth. I can't believe you strung me along for so long,' he said, shaking his head. 'You played me for a right fool. But, you know what? I'm not the fool here—you are.'

He looked her up and down one last time before snarling his last judgement. 'You're pathetic.'

And then he turned and strode out of the door.

Daniel's team kept out of his way the following day. Every time he entered a room in the tropical plant nursery it wouldn't exactly empty immediately, but after about ten minutes of concentrated work he'd look up to find himself totally alone. He was so angry he couldn't see straight.

Much more so than when Georgia had made her stupid proposal. He understood now that his ex's actions had been a combination of a ticking biological clock mixed with a healthy dose of panic. It had been a daft reflex action, and he could forgive her for that.

But Chloe...

Chloe had lied.

He'd thought he'd been so clever, carefully reeling her in, when all along it had been the other way around. She wasn't an orchid at all. She was a sneaky, twisting, climbing weed.

There was a cracking sound and he realised he'd been gripping a square plastic pot a little too tightly. That was the third one today. For punishment he threw it across the nursery.

There was a flash of movement near the door, and he turned to find Alan standing there, waving a blue and white checked tea towel above his head.

'What are you doing?' Daniel barked.

Alan stopped waving and let his arm drop to his side. 'It was the closest I could find to a white flag,' he muttered.

'Don't be ridiculous!' Daniel said. He hadn't been that bad, had he?

'I have staff volunteering for manure duty,' Alan said, 'just so they can get out of here for the afternoon. What the hell is wrong with you?'

Daniel just gave him a thunderous look.

Alan nodded knowingly. 'Ah, woman trouble.' He put the tea towel down on the bench near the door and walked over to Daniel. 'What's Fancy Knickers done now?'

'Shut up, Alan,' Daniel said.

He didn't want to think about Chloe. Especially not

combined with the phrase Fancy Knickers. He'd been having rogue flashbacks enough as it was, and he didn't want to prompt any more.

Too late.

An image of her leaning over him as he sat on the sofa, a pale thigh either side of his jeans, and the ring-side view of just what a good bra could do for a cleavage assaulted him.

He batted the image away, attempting to replace it with the tacky-leaved *Drosera* on the bench in front of him. It wasn't much competition, really. His mind started to slide in the wrong direction once again.

He made himself focus on the plant. *Remember,* he told himself, *they're both the same really—covered in sweetness that promises heaven but is really a fatal trap.* One he'd only just survived before. Nothing on earth would tempt him to go back there again.

'Have you seen her today?' he asked Alan. Daniel hadn't. Which meant she'd had the good sense to keep out of his way.

Alan shook his head. 'She didn't come in this morning.'

That just stoked Daniel's anger further. Not just a liar but a coward, too.

'What did she do, mate?' Alan asked. 'It has to be pretty monumental to get you in this state.'

'She… She…'

What *had* she done?

His brain flooded with images from the night before: Chloe, sweet and sexy, half naked and responsive beneath his hands… Her easy smile and that killer body… That darn tiny hook at the top of her dress.

He opened his mouth and then shut it again. Telling Alan she'd invited him back to her place, stripped down to the most eye-popping lingerie he'd ever seen and then had tried to seduce him just didn't sound very awful. Alan definitely wouldn't understand.

In fact, at the mercy of the movie reel of memories inside his own head, Daniel was finding it harder to understand it himself.

But then another image in his brain came sharply into focus—the photograph that had been hidden in the book—and suddenly his anger came flooding back.

She'd promised him one thing and then had delivered him something else entirely.

Promised you?

Yes. Promised him. With every wiggle of her hips, with every cool and casual comment, every retreat when he'd advanced. She'd made him believe they were the same, that they wanted the same thing. And it hadn't been true at all.

He could have slept with her anyway, but that wasn't his style, and he knew it would have been a mistake. Those tendrils, like jungle creepers, would have started to wind around him, to suffocate him.

'It's complicated,' he told Alan. 'You know women.'

Alan nodded sagely.

'I'll be fine in a while,' Daniel told him. 'I just need to let off some steam first.'

Alan chuckled. 'The rate you're going, we can just turn the misters and the heating off and let you regulate the nursery single-handed.'

Daniel let out a reluctant laugh.

Alan walked back over to the door. 'That's the problem with women. We want to chase them, but we then have to deal with them when we catch them.'

You did all the chasing...

Chloe's words from the evening before echoed round his head. He had chased her. He'd chased hard. The fact she was right only made him more angry.

But that had been part of his downfall. He'd been so busy trying to break down her barriers that he hadn't realised he hadn't been tending his own.

He picked up the *Drosera* and inspected it closely. Tiny black flies decorated its sticky leaves.

Stupid man, he told himself. *Because you thought she was safe, that she didn't want diamonds and confetti and wedding rings, you let yourself like her.* Because he had genuinely liked being with her. It hadn't all been about getting her into bed.

He hadn't wanted her to be one of those clingy, silly women who just threw themselves at him. He'd wanted to spend time with her, have a wild and crazy affair that lasted as long as it lasted. And who wouldn't? Because, despite how she'd acted in the past, the Chloe Michaels of today was clever and funny and sexy, and she'd reminded him of who he'd used to be before...

A chill settled over him. Maybe that was why. Maybe, even though he hadn't realised it, because she was from that time in his life when he was really happy, he'd recognised that on some subconscious level, been drawn to it.

Which meant he had to stay away from her now. He didn't want any memories of that time. Because remembering the good years meant remembering what came after. And it had taken him too long travelling the world, seeking adventure to make him forget.

He was good at forgetting. At blocking out.

And now he had one more thing to block out from his life—Chloe Michaels.

Chloe was very glad that the day after her sickie was a Saturday and she wasn't due to go in to work. She did better than the previous day, where she'd mostly sat in the cramped space between her bed and her chest of drawers, her back to the wall, and cried. She made it out of her bedroom and into the living room. Not for long, though. Every stick of furniture in her room seemed to have some link with Thursday night.

The problem with living so close to the botanical gardens was that she was scared to go outside in case she met someone from work. In the end, she resorted to desperate measures and rang her parents to say she was coming home for the weekend for a surprise visit.

Mum and Dad were just as they always were. They looked after her, they fed her cups of tea and short-cake—which was all lovely—but then there were the dinner-table conversations. How pleased they were that she was working somewhere as prestigious as Kew, even if was just looking after one tiny section. Never mind. In a few years she could go for promotion and really do something.

Chloe wanted to tell them she was doing something, that she loved her job and didn't yearn for corporate headship, or knighthood—or sainthood—whatever it was they wanted for her, but she didn't have the energy.

Besides, if they kept on about her professional life they wouldn't ask about her personal life.

It had started a couple of years ago. First the veiled questions, but they'd grown less and less subtle. Had she met anyone nice? Was anyone serious about her? Of course, she'd always looked better with longer hair so maybe she should grow it out, and she'd do well not to forget that it was all downhill after thirty and they really wanted some grandchildren while her eggs were still good.

They meant well, they really did.

But Chloe didn't need a reminder that her personal life was going down the toilet. At least, if her parents kept on about work, she'd avoid having to tell them it had been her who'd pulled the chain.

But Monday would not be put off for ever.

She woke before dawn and stared at her ceiling, listening to the planes coming in to land at Heathrow, her stomach churning. She really didn't want to go in. She couldn't face it, couldn't face seeing him, especially after what he'd said to her.

You're pathetic.

Those words had lodged in her chest like an arrow's shaft and would not be shaken loose.

She *was* pathetic. What serious, grown-up horticulturist fantasised about taking a taxi to the airport, buying a one-way ticket and just getting on a plane? Any plane. As long as it took her thousands of miles away.

Five months. That was all she'd had in her dream job before it had turned into a nightmare.

Even though it was not yet six, Chloe dragged herself out of bed and made herself get dressed. Lying there feeling sorry for herself was not going to help. She needed to get ready, get some serious armour in place if she was going to survive today, both physical and emotional. If there was one thing she was not going to give up it was her job. Daniel Bradford would just have to deal with that.

She'd chosen her usual confidence-boosting uniform of pink blouse and black skirt, but when she opened her wardrobe to look for matching shoes she realised they were still under her bed where she'd kicked them off after Daniel had left. She staggered back from the open wardrobe and her bottom met the end of the bed with a bump. For a few seconds, she stared straight ahead, but then she reached underneath the bed and her fingers closed around the hard and spiky heel of a pink stiletto. She pulled it out and stared at it.

She didn't ever want to wear those shoes again. She certainly didn't want to wear them today. Daniel would just think she was sending him some creepy, stalker-type message or something. The man was paranoid.

And vain. And arrogant.

And so gorgeous she couldn't think straight.

How—after all he'd said to her, after how he'd made her feel—could she still be attracted to him? Daniel Bradford was right. She *was* pathetic. She needed to get herself a life, and she needed to do it fast.

Which, unfortunately, meant she really was going to have to get up off her backside and go to work today. Because work was all she had left at the moment.

She threw the pink heel into the back of her wardrobe, plucked its twin from under the bed and did the same, then pulled out some less spectacular black shoes with a lower heel. They were comfortable, though, she thought as she slid her feet into them, which would be good, because she'd bet those shoes were the only thing that was going to be comfortable about her working day today.

NINE

———

Chloe walked into the tropical nurs-
eries with her head held high and went straight to her
section, looking neither to the left nor the right. She
didn't care where Daniel was. If she ran into him, she
ran into him. But she wasn't going to give the other
staff a show by confronting him. She knew what they
called her behind her back, but today she was going to
be *Classy Knickers* instead of *Fancy Knickers*.

She reached her section and began checking out the
various orchids she was propagating. Still that one
Paphiopedilum she'd grown from an unidentified seed
refused to flower, no matter what she did. She'd noticed
from the package that it had come from Georgia Stone
at the Millennium Seed Bank. Daniel's ex.

Perhaps it was absorbing all her pent up guilt at wanting him after he'd ditched the other woman so publicly.
Georgia needn't worry, though. Now Chloe was part of
the same exclusive club. As humiliating as being turned
down live on air must have been, at least she hadn't
been wearing just her underwear. Underwear suppos-

edly guaranteed to provoke an entirely different reaction in the male of the species.

Chloe shook her head and tried to banish those thoughts by searching for tips on the Internet and emailing other enthusiasts, but she couldn't lose herself in her work as she normally did. Every sense—especially her hearing—was on full alert. In the backstage area of her brain she was straining to hear his deep, rich voice. And whatever it was that was working overtime just didn't seem to have an off switch.

In the end she gave up trying. Every sound had her jumping out of her skin. As much as she told herself she didn't care if she saw him, she really did. She was just dreading seeing that same look of disgust in his eyes, telling her she was pointless and pathetic.

She decided to get some fresh air, go down to the Princess of Wales Conservatory and check on her orchids. There was something soothing about the two rooms filled with logs and ferns and perfect flowers. She and Daniel had discussed doing a joint display around the little boggy pool in the Temperate Orchid section—long-fluted pitcher plants mixed with delicate woodland orchids—but that obviously wasn't going to happen now, so she might as well head down there and get some new ideas.

Walking back through the network of nurseries to the entrance was skin-crawlingly embarrassing. Not many people had seen her arrive, but now word must have gone round because they were certainly watching her leave. Every time she passed a door the noise level dropped as those inside stopped what they were doing.

It only made her tip her chin higher, straighten her spine further.

They'd be calling her *Iron Knickers* by the end of the day, because she'd be blasted if she'd let any of them see her crumble. It had been bad enough to have Daniel witness her steady disintegration. She didn't need their pity. Didn't want it.

The short walk to the conservatory was like an oasis in a desert of stress. Though there were a handful of Kew employees around, they were rolling wheelbarrows or chopping down trees. None of them stopped and stared. The gossip obviously hadn't reached the tree gang or the bedding crew yet, but it would.

She'd walked via the quieter paths to the south entrance of the glasshouse, and then she zigzagged down its angular paths, keeping to the side routes as much as possible. She was within feet of one of the orchid enclosures when she saw a figure she recognised coming from the offices hidden under the earth and foliage.

Emma. But instead of saying something totally inappropriate, the other woman merely laid a sympathetic hand on her arm. 'How are you doing?'

The contact seemed to burn like acid. Chloe had a sudden and horrifying flashback to the day the woman in the raincoat had pounced on Daniel. They were standing in almost exactly the same spot where she'd rubbed the woman's arm and spoke comforting words. Never in a million years had Chloe expected to be on the receiving end of the same pitying looks.

Poor Chloe. Just another one of Drop-Dead Daniel's corpses...

She stiffened under Emma's touch. 'Okay.'

The other woman studied her face. 'Really?'

Chloe's stomach dropped like a plummeting lift and she nodded dumbly. 'I don't really want to talk about it,' she said scratchily.

Emma just nodded sympathetically and returned to her work. None of the usual platitudes, but that wasn't really Emma. Nothing about the healing properties of time, or alternative fishing locations. Nothing about Chloe being too good for him anyway.

Because everyone knew that wasn't true.

Especially Daniel.

She walked stiffly to the plate glass door that led to the orchid enclosure, relishing the climate-controlled cool air on her skin after the humidity of the Wet Tropics zone. Once there she stared into one of the display cases—rarer specimens protected by a wall of glass—and exhaled.

She'd been so stupid, hadn't she?

For a decade she'd been turning herself into a turbo-charged, bionic version of herself, determined to never be the sort of woman a man like Daniel could ever reject, and it hadn't worked.

He'd run from the frizzy-haired mouse.

He'd also run from New Chloe. Twice as fast.

She didn't know what to do now, didn't know who to be. Her best just hadn't been good enough, not by a long shot, and she didn't have the energy to build better and higher. Not yet.

She turned around, pressed her back against the glass and let her knees buckle under her until she was crouching on the floor. The display across the enclosure was beautiful, rocks and logs, dripping with colourful blooms. It was like salve to her jagged emotions.

Perhaps she would just be the girl who loved orchids for a while, the girl who loved their fragile and ostentatious beauty, because, at the moment, it was the only thing she thought she was good at.

Chloe stood nervously outside Daniel's smart black door and looked for somewhere to place the gift bag in her hands so she could disappear back into the twilight. Somewhere Kelly would see it if she opened the door or came back home, but not somewhere inviting enough that someone on the street might see it and pinch it.

There was a small alcove on one side of the small tiled porch, offering some cover from anyone walking along the pavement. She was just reaching over to place the bag on the floor next to some empty milk bottles when the door opened—just a notch. Chloe froze.

She looked up to find Cal blinking at her. She pressed a finger to her lips, began to back away, but he suddenly threw his head back and yelled, 'There's someone at the door,' in the full-volumed way only a four-year-old could.

Chloe barely had time to back away before the door was yanked wide and she was staring at a broad, T-shirted chest.

Oh, poop.

She hadn't seen him much since that night on her boat. A glimpse of him here and there over the last week, always glaring at her, as if she had no right to be in *his* nursery, be one of *his* staff. It had got right on her nerves.

And then everything had gone quiet. People at work had seemed to relax a little, had stopped scanning the corridors when either she or Daniel was around, waiting for the other one to appear. When she'd told Emma, the other woman explained that Daniel had asked for emergency leave—something to do with his sister.

That news had made Chloe go cold all over. That could only mean one thing: Daniel was required to look after the boys because something had happened to Kelly. After his sister's recent health scares, she didn't even dare imagine what. It was too awful.

She and Daniel might not be getting along at the moment—she guffawed mentally at the understatement—but she liked Kelly, had admired how strong she seemed after all she'd been through. So she'd gone out and bought some pampering things, just some nice body lotion and some bath soak. The plan had been to pop it on the doorstep and sneak away before anyone spotted her.

The plan had obviously been flawed.

He folded his arms across his chest. 'What in hell's name are you doing here?' he said in a low, menacing whisper.

'I... Ah...'

Body not working. Brain not working. Lips definitely not working. She was going for the full house here.

Instead she dived for the bag, meaning to just take it and flee, but unfortunately Daniel lunged for it at the same time and their skulls produced a beautiful clear cracking sound as they made contact. Chloe staggered back, clutching her crown. Daniel, however, must have had an iron-capped skull, because he didn't seem to be in quite as much pain, although the swear word he uttered was very colourful.

Then a little voice from behind his knees repeated it beautifully, with the same intonation and gusto.

'Cal,' he said, and she could hear the strain that told her he was hanging onto his last thread of patience, 'just go back inside and see what Ben is up to, will you?'

'Okay, Uncle Daniel,' the voice said chirpily, and then Chloe could hear him skipping off down the hall, testing his new word out all the way.

Still holding her head, she straightened and came eye to eye with a rather angry Daniel Bradford. Good. She was angry too.

Angry at being made to feel like a pariah in her workplace. Angry that every time he'd set eyes on her since that night he'd looked as if he'd like to set fire to her with his glare. Angry that he hadn't let her explain, and that she'd known instinctively that he wouldn't have listened.

'I asked you a question,' he growled.

Chloe smoothed her T-shirt down with her free hand. 'I was just dropping these off for—'

He made a dismissive gesture towards the bag in her hand but, unfortunately, the edge of his hand caught it and the bottles went flying. His first reaction was shock, but then his expression hardened again. 'I don't want anything you've got to give me.'

Unfortunately, since Chloe had bought Kelly some rather nice lotions, the bottles were glass not plastic. One bounced on the small lawn, but the other one hit the path and smashed.

'Now look what you've done!' she shouted.

She knew it was pointless, but she reached out to pick up the bits from amidst the fragrant, snowy white lotion now oozing into the dirt. She couldn't leave it there. One of the boys might tread on it.

'You really are unhinged, aren't you?' a superior voice said from above her. 'I had no idea how bad it was.'

'Listen, you egotistical jerk—ow!' Chloe flinched away as her fingertip met glass. Instinctively, she stuck her finger in her mouth but instantly spat it out again. That lotion definitely did not taste as good as it smelled.

He let out a frustrated sigh. 'I'm sorry you've hurt yourself, but this can't continue...I don't need any of your gifts. And I don't want you hanging around outside my house.'

Chloe's lips twitched, then a high-pitched laugh burst out of her mouth. And once she'd started she couldn't stop. She clamped her good hand over her mouth to muffle the noise. This man was priceless! He actually thought she was *stalking* him? Just how vain could a man get?

She looked up at him, the look of twisted confusion on his features at her sudden outburst, and that just made her laugh all the harder.

When she could finally manage a sentence in one go, she said, 'This wasn't for you, Daniel. It was for Kelly.'

The look of astonishment on his face was almost worth the pain in her finger.

'For Kelly...' he repeated slowly.

'Yes,' said Chloe, feeling her hilarity subside and her temper rise again. 'You know—tall, dark-haired female who lives with you and shares a gene pool, God help her.'

'Why...?' he said. 'Why are you bringing presents for
Kelly? It's not her birthday.'

A week ago, if she'd seen Daniel Bradford rendered
defenceless by confusion like this, she'd have thought
it was sweet. Now Chloe just revelled in it. He was so
full of himself, thought he knew who she was and what
she was capable of, did he?

'I heard you'd had to take leave because of Kelly,' she
said. 'I thought she might be...well, you know, that she
might have found out...' She shoved the undamaged
bottle in Daniel's direction. 'Look, I just thought she
might need some girly pampering to cheer her up, okay?
It's hardly a crime.'

His mouth worked. 'But I thought...'

'Yes, I know what you thought,' she said. 'And, believe me, I've got much better things to do with my time
than stalk you. You made it abundantly clear you're not
interested.'

Daniel's gaze drifted to her finger. The blob of lotion on her hand was now looking like raspberry-ripple
ice cream, with a swirl of red amongst the thick white.
'You'd better come inside.'

Chloe shook her head. 'Not likely. I'm not giving you
any more ammunition than I have already. Next thing
I know you'll have the police down here.'

'Don't be idiotic,' he said, regaining some of his usual
charm.

Chloe started to laugh again, a dry, airless sound.
'You've destroyed your sister's gift and accused me of
stalking you, and *I'm* the one who's idiotic?'

He folded his arms again. 'Well, after the other
night...'

'For goodness' sake! All I did was get a little friendly with a man I *thought* was interested. And now I'm a stalker? Haven't you ever made a pass at the wrong person before? It didn't make you an evil monster, did it?'

His mouth moved, but Chloe was very satisfied to discover that he had no words to rebut her valid argument. It just spurred her on.

'And, up until that moment, I didn't hear you complaining one bit. Quite the reverse.'

He glared down at her. 'Are you quite finished?'

Chloe sucked in air through her nostrils and let it out through her mouth. 'Actually, I think I am.' And she was feeling much better now.

Daniel was staring at her finger again. It was starting to drip.

'I really think you'd better come inside,' he said.

Looking at her finger, Chloe did too. 'Okay. But as long as you understand that it's only for medical attention and you will in no way be applying for a restraining order if I step foot over that threshold for a few minutes.'

His eyes narrowed. 'Done.'

So Chloe gathered up her courage, and her pride, and followed him inside.

Daniel fetched the first-aid kit from the kitchen cupboard and placed it on the kitchen table, thereby avoiding any need for physical contact. Whose benefit that was for, he wasn't sure. Despite Chloe's recent behaviour, his brain had not got the message through to his libido that she was better left alone. What business did she have looking so soft and approachable, even when she was staring up at him defiantly and telling him just how badly he'd got it wrong?

'There are plasters and disinfectant in there,' he said.

Chloe gave him a withering look. 'I haven't lost my IQ in the last week, you know,' she said. 'I have a fairly good grasp on the contents of a first-aid kit.'

Daniel squeezed his teeth together and said nothing.

Chloe ran her finger under the tap, attempting to clean the thick lotion away so she could see the damage. 'It's not very deep,' she said, moving it back and forth under the stream of water, 'just bleeding impressively. A plaster should do it.'

Daniel handed her a clean towel. She took it without looking at him. As she dried her finger she shook her head gently.

'We spent a lot of time together over the last couple of months, but you don't know me at all.'

'That's hardly surprising, since you were pretending to be something you're not.'

Much to his surprise, Chloe laughed softly. 'No, I wasn't. I just didn't look like the silly nineteen-year-old you remembered, but I'm still the same person on the inside. You didn't look deep enough—now or then—to see the truth.' She dabbed her finger with the towel, decorating it with tiny red smears. 'You were just fixated on the outside package. You didn't care what was underneath. And you're *still* fixated on the outside package. All you can see now is one of those silly women who follow you around, and I'm not one of them, either.'

A look of relief washed over her face as she said that last sentence. She inhaled and the hint of a smile played on her lips.

Daniel frowned. He didn't want to think about whether she was right about that. Anyway, she hadn't acted perfectly in the situation, either. 'You should have been upfront and honest with me, right from the start. It would have stopped me—'

She laughed. 'What? Making a fool of yourself? Welcome to the club, Daniel.'

He supposed she had him there. However stupid he must have felt knowing he hadn't realised who she was, she must have felt ten times as bad when he'd stormed off her boat the previous week.

'Why hide it?' he asked. 'If you were okay with it?'

She checked her finger and clamped the towel back around it. 'I didn't.' She looked down at the red-flecked towel, and then she met his eyes. 'At least, I didn't plan to. That first day when I came to find you, I was making a pre-emptive strike. I'd planned to 'fess up and make light of it, let you know I'd grown up and moved on... But you didn't remember me. As far as I knew, you didn't remember that night either.'

'So you lied.'

Chloe shook her head and sighed. 'Oh, how wonderful it must be to live in that perfect black-and-white world of yours. I didn't lie, I just decided not to dredge it up if you'd forgotten the whole thing. How would you have reacted if I'd said: "Hi, Daniel! Remember that tubby student who launched herself at you a few years back? That was me! Aren't you thrilled?"'

Okay, he kind of saw her point.

She pulled the towel away from her hand and inspected the cut. It wasn't oozing any more, so, forgetting about the *not touching* thing, Daniel reached for a plaster, unpeeled its wrapper and stuck it over the cut, winding the ends firmly round her finger.

Chloe didn't say anything while he did this, but when he stepped away again she said, 'I just thought the past could stay in the past, where it belonged—neither of us are the same people we were back then—and that we could work together as sensible adults. That was my plan, and I stuck to it. It was you who tipped everything on its head!'

Daniel straightened and stared at her. 'Me?'

That twinkle of humour that he now recognised as a precursor to one of Chloe's stinging truths appeared in her eyes. 'Yes, *you*, Indiana. Who was it who decided to kiss me in the Palm House, to flirt with me continually? Who was it that was trying to woo me?'

'I did not *woo*,' he said, slightly affronted. That term made him think of lovesick idiots who couldn't help themselves.

'Yes, you certainly did woo. What was that picnic about, then? Or the cosy dinner with your family to get me to let my guard down...?' She saw the expression on his face and carried on vindicated. 'Oh, yes, I'm wise to the way you operate now, and you can't chalk all that up as my desperate behaviour. I didn't engineer any of those things, you did. You know what...?'

He wasn't really sure he did want to know, but she was on a roll now.

'In fact,' she said, 'if I was a man and you were a woman, you'd be the stalker and I'd be the stud. How fair is that?'

Not fair at all. But Daniel wasn't going to tell her that. Not when he was remembering just how much he had *wooed*. Just how much he hadn't been able to help himself, how desperate he'd been to make her his. In the physical sense, of course. It had nothing to do with her bright personality and quick humour, the way he felt lighter—freer—when he was with her.

Chloe inspected her finger and seemed pleased with it. She zipped the little green first-aid kit back up and put it on the table with a slight lift of one eyebrow. Copying him. Mocking him.

'I'm not obsessed with you,' she said. 'And rest assured I will not attempt to seduce you ever again.'

Why did his body tighten in response to her words, rather than back away?

'I think it's a good idea if we just steer clear of each other from now on,' she added.

'Okay.' Daniel nodded, but he didn't really like that idea for some reason. There'd been a great deal of satisfaction in striding round the tropical plant nursery like a bear with a sore head, feeling the injured party. It had blocked out all those niggling little regrets he'd had about that night: how he'd spoken to her. Even worse, how he wished he'd stayed...

'Let's just be calm and professional. That way everyone at work can go back to minding their own business again—no drama to see—and we can get on with our jobs and our lives.'

'Okay...'

Her brow wrinkled, and Daniel couldn't help remember how, when she'd been sitting on his lap, all but naked, she'd made the same face as his lips trailed down her neck and across her shoulder, how it had seemed she'd been lost in concentrating on every touch and taste.

'It sounds as if there's a *but* in there somewhere.'

'No,' he said, mildly confused with all the conflicting messages his body and brain were sending him. One was saying run; one was telling him to make her make that slightly pained look of pleasure again. 'It's just that I'm not used to—'

'Women being so reasonable around you?' she interjected saucily. 'Using their silly heads instead of being ramped up on their hormones and acting desperate?'

She waited for him to answer, but he didn't want to give her the satisfaction.

'I know you've had to put up with some weird behaviour since Valentine's Day,' she said, her demeanour softening slightly, 'but, honestly, you need to get over yourself. Not every woman you meet wants to marry you, Daniel. But, one day, somebody might, and if you don't calm down you're going to scare her off.'

He shook his head. 'I'm never getting married,' he said emphatically. Maybe too emphatically, because Chloe suddenly looked at him with a mixture of realisation and pity. He hated the pity the most. But he needn't have worried. It quickly clouded over with a darker emotion.

'Then you're a coward as well as a bighead,' she said. Ouch.

'What is the big, bad, adventuring Daniel Bradford scared of?'

'Nothing,' he said blandly.

She backed away towards the door. 'Now who's the liar?' she said softly. 'Okay, I got it wrong—I made a move on the wrong person—but at least I had the guts to try. I made myself vulnerable, took a chance. I'll never find the right man for me if I don't.'

He must have had horror written all over his face at her words, because he saw her read him, saw her muscles tighten and her jaw clench.

'Yes, I want to get married...some day,' she said, lifting her chin. 'What's so wrong with that? Millions of people do every year. But you...' The look she gave him made his insides wither. It reminded him of another look, another woman, another barrage of accusations he hadn't been able to defend himself against. Rather than crumble under the weight of them, Daniel fired up his temper to match hers.

'You,' she continued, her voice shaking slightly, 'you're too scared to even try. A wedding ring won't melt your finger like acid, you know! One conquest after the next... Is that really what you want? Does that really make you happy?'

No! he wanted to yell at her.

So he did.

'No, but I've been down the other path and I'm not going back there!'

There was a flicker of hesitation in her self-righteous expression and it fuelled him further. He couldn't let her be right about everything, couldn't let her make him seem shallow and pathetic.

'What do you mean?' she asked, 'What "other path"?'

He marched over to her, stared her down, let her know he wasn't scared of her and her words. He'd lived through far worse. 'I mean,' he said, his voice low and silky, 'that I once had a wife and a son. I did the whole marriage thing, the whole 'til-death-do-us-part thing and it didn't work out so well.'

When he mentioned the word *death* her lashes blinked rapidly and she swallowed. 'She died?' she asked, barely more than whispering.

'No,' Daniel said, turning away, hardly able to look at Chloe again. He hated the fact that a tiny voice had piped up inside his head, telling him it might have been better that way. 'No, it was until "death do us part" but it wasn't hers.' His voice dried and he had to swallow to get it back. 'My son. Cot death. Six months old.'

He turned back to Chloe. He'd thought he'd feel vindicated, but the look of complete shock on her face actually made him feel a little queasy. He could tell she was searching for words. There weren't any. He knew that for a fact.

'Something as fragile as a marriage can't handle that,' he said. 'I wasn't even there...I was off in some jungle, being the big explorer.'

He let out a huff of dry laughter.

'She never forgave me, you know. It killed everything we had. So, no, I don't want to get married again. Excuse me for that.'

Chloe's eyes filled with tears. She swallowed them down, stepped forward and reached for him. 'Oh, Daniel...I'm so sorry.'

He shook his head, backed away until his backside met the counter. He didn't want her pity. 'Thank you for Kelly's present,' he said calmly. 'She's fine, by the way. A last-minute opportunity to go on a training course that she couldn't pass up. Nothing to worry about.' He looked at the paper bag with its drooping string handles, still where he'd left it in the centre of the kitchen table. 'If you'll tell me where you got it, I'll replace the broken one.'

She shook her head.

So she didn't want to owe him anything now, not even that. Maybe it was for the best.

'Daniel...'

He turned to stare out of the window, down the garden. 'You're right,' he said. 'Let's just steer clear of each other. Calm and professional.'

For a long time she didn't move; he could hear her breathing softly, a slight catch in the rhythm now and then. He screwed up his face, desperately trying to hold onto the churning chaos inside that he'd called up with his admission. Eventually, he heard the rustle of the paper bag as she lifted it off the table, her heels on the tiled hallway, the soft thud of the front door being closed gently.

And then Daniel let go of the breath he'd been holding and did something he hadn't done in years. He cried.

TEN

———

    And that was what Daniel and Chloe did for the next few months, through the bright days of August, the balmy warmth of an Indian Summer and into the rusts and golds of October. They steered clear of each other. Not too much, of course, because that would have created even more tension and gossip, but they were cordial and professional and those around them eventually lost interest.

Chloe also discovered a pleasing side effect of being Daniel's supposed ex—her nickname died out, and some of the female staff who'd previously kept their distance made an effort to befriend her, asked her out after work sometimes. It seemed everyone had a story to tell about a failed crush on Daniel Bradford. She and Georgia weren't the only members of that club. But with her credentials, Chloe thought she should be president. Or possibly queen...

But maybe it also had something to do with the fact that, as the trees lost their leaves, Chloe also shed some of her less practical work clothes. She swapped skirts

for trousers, left the uncomfortable shoes for the week-
ends. One morning she'd just found herself staring in
the mirror, red lipstick in hand. What was the point
now? Who was she trying to impress?

Not Daniel, even though he was constantly in her
thoughts.

She couldn't stop thinking about what he'd told her.
No wonder he avoided anything approaching intimacy.
No wonder a woman who looked as if she might cling on
and never let go was a threat. She understood it all now.
And she ached for him because, while she understood it,
she knew he was closing every open door around himself, and one day he'd wake up old and lonely. It was a
sad future for a man who was so energetic and fearless
in other areas of his life, a man who had such passion.

One morning Chloe checked her email before starting
work and found a message from Kew's PR team. She'd
been summoned to a meeting regarding the upcoming
orchid festival. Every February, when the grounds outside were still grey and brown, when only the tips of the
first crocuses were pushing through the grass, the Princess of Wales Conservatory became a riot of colour and
beauty. Chloe had been looking forward to it all year; it
would be her chance to really shine, show her superiors
what she could do. And she desperately needed something in her life to go right at the moment.

At the appointed hour, she made her way to the PR offices and knocked on Sarah Milton's door. When she entered the office, however, she got a surprise. She wasn't
the only one who'd been summoned. Daniel was also
there, sitting in one of the chairs opposite Sarah's desk.

Chloe shook Sarah's hand, smiling, and then did the

same to Daniel, figuring it would look odd if she treated him differently. It had been the first time they'd really touched since that awful night on her houseboat, and she'd hoped that all residual attraction would have faded by now.

She couldn't have been more wrong.

Instead, her skin leapt to life, tingling all the way up her arm. As if her nerve-endings had been lying dormant, waiting for something to wake them up. Waiting for *him* to wake them up.

She sat down in the remaining vacant chair and folded her hands in her lap.

Sarah, an elegant woman in her late forties, smiled at both of them and leaned forward on her desk, lacing her fingers together. 'I heard the two of you had plans for a combined display in the Princess of Wales,' she said, raising her eyebrows slightly.

She and Daniel looked at each other, then back at Sarah. 'Yes, but we kind of...put it on hold,' Chloe said.

The minuscule nod of Sarah's head said she knew that—and exactly why.

'We'd like you to resurrect the idea for this year's orchid festival in February,' she said. 'We're thinking of calling the festival something like "Beauty and the Beast" or "Savage Beauty". It'll be great for PR to do something a little different this year.'

Chloe sneaked a look at Daniel. His expression told her just how enthused he was by that idea.

'The last thing I need is more media attention,' he said.

Sarah just smiled at him, a long, thin, lizard's smile.

'Well, it's not really about you, is it, Daniel? It's supposed to be about the plants.'

Daniel just glared back at her.

Chloe found she just couldn't sit there and say nothing. 'I know it *should* be about the plants, but we all know the media will get any story they can out of it, the juicier the better. You have to admit that Daniel will be a target.'

Now Daniel was glaring at her instead. Great.

Sarah, however, wasn't fazed. 'We're going to run the festival for a week, with an auction for some of the display pieces on the last day to raise money for the Kew foundation,' she said. 'So book the fourteenth off in your diaries.'

'The *fourteenth*?' she and Daniel said in unison.

Daniel shook his head. 'But that's exactly one year on from—'

'Look, there's going to be media interest anyway,' Sarah said quickly. 'We might as well do it on our terms. What do you think?'

Chloe exhaled. What did she think about it? She loved the idea, knowing that the orchids and pitcher plants would look amazing together, but it would mean working with Daniel. She tipped her head a little and looked across at him again. His expression was unreadable, features set like stone. But saying no to the powers that be on her very first festival would not go down well. She'd waited years for this job, and she didn't want to jeopardise her future here by being labelled as difficult.

'I think we can make it work,' she said, knowing that Daniel had just transferred his caustic gaze from Sarah to her once again. She turned and met him head-on. 'There's no reason we can't work calmly together.'

'I'm glad to hear it,' Sarah said, looking a little smug. 'Daniel?'

Chloe leaned forward a little, towards Daniel. He watched her, but didn't move back. 'She's right, you know. About the media. At least this way you can talk about the plants, get some good media coverage for the gardens... Do a good enough job of it and no one is going to have time to ask you about your love life.'

At least, that was what Chloe was hoping. Especially as she'd been the one blip on his radar all year—as far as she knew.

Something in his eyes changed. 'Okay,' he said, looking back at Sarah.

'Great,' Sarah said, reaching for her mouse and giving her computer screen a glance. They were effectively dismissed. 'I'll leave you two to work out some more details, then we'll catch up again in a couple of weeks to see how things are coming along.'

Daniel worked his way through the Orangery restaurant to a table in the corner. Chloe was already there, head bent over a notepad. She couldn't possibly have heard him through the dull hum of afternoon tea, but she lifted her head and looked at him while he was still ten feet away.

'Hi,' she said.

He nodded in return.

Her voice had been calm and even, her expression neutral, but he sensed she was more nervous than she was letting on.

It was strange. It was as if Chloe were a two-way mirror and, for a long time, all he'd been able to see was what she reflected back to him on the surface. But someone had now switched a switch somewhere or turned a light on, and suddenly he could see everything she'd been hiding behind. Was it just that he hadn't been looking properly before? Could he have seen this all along if only he'd tried?

She wore dark jeans, boots and a sweatshirt. Her hair was still curled as usual, but she hardly looked as if she had any make-up on at all. She looked fresh and young, an odd mix of the woman he'd pursued so relentlessly and the student who'd got her timing wrong. How he hadn't recognised her the instant he'd seen her again, he didn't know.

He sat down. 'Do you want another drink?'

She shook her head, even though her cup was nearly empty. 'No, I'm fine.'

'So...Beauty and the Beast...' He shrugged. 'I reckon we all know who's who in that scenario.'

Her lips flattened and her brows lowered. 'We've managed just fine for months without any name-calling—'

He shook his head, leaned forward a little. 'I didn't mean *you* were the Beast,' he said. 'I thought it was obvious I was talking about me...that you were the...' He trailed off and didn't finish his sentence. Coward.

'Oh,' she said, and the resulting confusion on her face made her look younger still, very much like the girl he remembered. 'That's very... Thank you.'

She stared down at her notebook for a second.

'You're not...flirting...with me, are you? Because I don't think that's a good idea.'

He hadn't meant to, but then he hadn't meant to say anything like that at all. It had just popped out. 'No,' he said. 'It was just my backhanded way of saying I didn't handle things very well back in the summer.' He shrugged. 'You've met my sister, so you know subtlety is not a strong family trait.'

That earned him the beginnings of a smile. He could live with that.

What surprised him was the tug inside telling him it wasn't enough, that he wanted to see her eyes light up and her lips stretch the way he had done before, back when things had been easy between them, back when she'd still been a potential *something* to him.

He decided to ignore it and gestured towards the sketch pad. 'You have some ideas?'

She nodded, but didn't flap it over to show him. Not yet. It took her a couple of seconds before she worked up the nerve. And he didn't blame her. He'd been a complete pig to her, belittled everything she was. He didn't have to lie, though, when he saw her sketches and notes; she had some really good ideas. Chloe was much more imaginative than he'd realised.

Oh, you realised. When her hands were on your chest and her teeth were nipping your neck, you knew just how creative she had the potential to be.

Daniel wiped that thought away. He shouldn't think about her that way any more.

Okay, he was in trouble already, because he couldn't seem to *stop* thinking about her that way nowadays. But he needed to try. If he didn't, he'd be facing a sexual harassment suit. No way was Chloe Michaels ever going to let him within touching distance of her ever again. And he was supposed to be pleased about that.

He pulled the tatty piece of paper out of his jeans pocket. It was stained and crumpled, even though he'd only scratched his ideas on it about an hour ago, nothing as neat as Chloe's little black book with the elastic strap and colour-coded markers.

For the next half-hour they talked designs and specimens, discussed how to use different areas of the vast Wet Tropics zone of the Princess of Wales Conservatory. It was usual to have a large display by the lily-pad pool, but Chloe had ideas about how to use some of the smaller nooks and crannies of the area too. Together they worked on an idea of contrasting the ugliest and most vicious-looking plants in the collection with the most fragile and colourful orchids. She wanted hanging displays and islands in the ponds, great towers of orchids in spiralling colours. It was going to look stunning.

Eventually, she closed her notebook and looked around. While they'd been talking a couple of the other nursery staff had wandered over to see what they were planning, but she'd always found a way to lean over her notebook or distract them from its contents. 'I want this to be a surprise,' she said. 'I know we'll need a huge team of helpers closer to the date, but for now I'd like to keep this just between ourselves.'

He couldn't help smiling a little. 'Need to know basis only. Got it. Anyone finds out too much and we *deal* with them.'

Her lips twitched. 'Exactly. There's some rather hungry piranhas in the aquatic display. I'm sure they'd appreciate the nutritional supplement.' And then she grew more serious again. 'I don't want you to take this the wrong way, Daniel, but... Do you think we could meet somewhere less...public...next time?'

'I'm not taking it the wrong way,' he said. How could he? For the last three months she'd been true to her word. She hadn't so much as looked at him with a flicker of interest. There'd been no text messages, no voicemails, no scented envelopes in the post. All completely what he'd asked for. So he shouldn't really mind, should he?

She'd moved on. Got over him. So maybe she was right: maybe he was big-headed, because he wasn't liking the fact it had been so easy for her. The fact that she'd dealt with the whole situation with poise and dignity—much more than he had—only made him admire her more.

But there was where the problem lay: usually, when he *admired* a woman, he let her know, he pursued her. He didn't quite know what to do with all these new, noble feelings he was having for Chloe that meant it wasn't going to end with a good night in bed. It was most unsettling.

'Okay,' he said. 'How about meeting at my house next Thursday?'

She opened her mouth and he could tell she was about to knock him back.

'I'll ask Kelly to hang around,' he added, knowing they'd struck up a friendship of late. 'She usually has some pithy opinions on my great plans.'

Chloe relaxed a little and nodded. 'Okay.'

'Okay.'

A cute little line appeared between her brows. 'We

can do this, can't we? We can act like professionals and
make this thing a success. Because I really want this
thing to be a success.'

He nodded. 'Sure.'

But as she walked away he drew in a deep breath and
held it. He made himself turn to the wall and look at
the white-painted plaster rather than at her rather fine
retreating backside in its denim covering.

See? He could do it. He was practically being a saint.

Okay. Well, he was going to try his best. That was all
anyone could ask.

Chloe closed her notebook, leaned back in one of
Daniel's dining-room chairs and sighed. 'Finally, I think
we have a handle on this thing,' she said, and then she
smiled, just a little. 'You know this is going to be the
best festival yet, don't you?'

Daniel grinned at her. Chloe smiled more than just
a little.

She lifted her tote bag off the floor and placed her
notebook inside before pushing her chair back, getting
ready to stand up. 'Wait?' he asked softly.

She dropped back down onto the chair.

'Before you go,' he said, 'I'd like to talk to you about
some things...clear the air.'

The air was clear as far as Chloe was concerned. Okay,
maybe not totally clear; Daniel's pheromones seemed
to be particularly strong this evening. But if they were
talking about their relationship—or non-relationship—
she was fine.

'It's okay. Really,' she said, flicking a loose ringlet out
of her eyes with a nod of her head.

'No, it isn't. I want to—need to—apologise for the things I said that night.'

Chloe blinked and her lids stayed shut a fraction too long. When she looked back at him, he was waiting, eyes intense, face serious. But there was an honesty, an openness, about him that she'd never seen before.

But it wasn't like those heated looks from the early days of their relationship. No, it was much more dangerous. This was the kind of look that made a woman ache for a man, somewhere deep, deep down inside, and Chloe was already too bruised in that place. She was also too weak to resist if he kept it up.

'I'm sorry I called you pathetic,' he said, his voice rough. 'I don't think you're pathetic at all. Far from it.'

She nodded. Her heart rate tripled.

'And you were right. I overreacted...'

Chloe licked her lips and twitched her shoulders in the slightest of shrugs. 'Maybe just a little,' she said dryly.

'What happened that night...'

She sat up straighter. 'I really don't want to rehash what went on at my houseboat—for all sorts of reasons.'

He looked down, then back up at her. 'No, I didn't mean *that* night. I meant the other one—back when you were a student.'

Chloe said something most unladylike. The only effect it had on Daniel was to make him laugh.

'Seriously, nothing to explain,' she said. 'I got a little tipsy, you offered to walk me outside for some fresh air and then I made a total and complete fool of myself by trying to kiss you. Believe me, after all these years it's crystal clear.'

She couldn't quite believe she'd said that, put it all so bluntly. And to Daniel, of all people. Why hadn't a large pit opened up in his kitchen floor and swallowed her whole?

'You were a student,' he said. 'It would have been completely unethical, even if I'd wanted to.'

Chloe swallowed hard and nodded. Yes, she'd known that. Hadn't stopped her doing it anyway. She'd never, ever drunk cheap cider again after that night. She tried to smile, but it felt more as if she was wincing. 'It's okay. You don't have to say that. I know you wouldn't have wanted to.' She broke eye contact with Daniel and looked away.

He was silent for a few seconds. 'I *shouldn't* have wanted to.'

She whipped her head round to stare at him. Why was he teasing her like that? He was supposed to be apologising, she thought, not making it worse.

'Daniel, so far you've been brutally honest about that...incident. You don't have to lie now. You didn't remember me at all.'

'I didn't make the connection,' he replied. 'And the details are still a little fuzzy, but I do remember an eager girl who always sat at the front for every lecture, who asked pertinent questions, who showed all the other students up with her passion and enthusiasm.'

Passion and enthusiasm? Was that another way of saying *huge crush on the teacher*? She folded her arms on the table in front of her and propped herself up with them. 'That girl was a joke.'

'No... She was sweet and young and had one too many,' he said. 'What student hasn't? But I should have handled that night better too.' He paused and frowned slightly. 'I probably would have, if it had just been any old sloppy drunken kiss.'

The look in his pale eyes made her hold her breath.

'You know we have great chemistry,' he said, his voice deepening. 'It was there then.'

Chloe shook her head slightly. That couldn't be. Yes, there had been fireworks and tingling and melting into a puddle at his feet, but that had been all her. It hadn't been him. He'd pushed her away, body rigid, eyes full of shock, eyes full of...

She looked back at him and he held her gaze.

Eyes full of surprise, with wide pupils—just as they were now—not pinpricks of disgust.

Oh.

She swallowed. That didn't change anything. He'd still done the right thing. If he hadn't he'd have lost his job and her reputation would have been even worse than it had been. At least no one had seen that drunken pass in the car park. At least they'd only teased her about her obvious crush.

She found she couldn't speak above a whisper. 'I don't know how that helps anything, but thank you for being honest with me.'

He exhaled. 'I don't know how it helps, either. I hadn't quite planned on saying it. But maybe it needed to be said.'

Chloe nodded. She wasn't sure if she agreed. It was hard to feel that distance between them now. She needed that distance. Because she had her own apology to give, her own admission to make.

But at that moment Kelly appeared in the doorway. 'Uncle Daniel's presence is required. Apparently,

Mummy cannot read *The Gruffalo* with all the right voices.'

Chloe stared at the table top. See? That was why she needed distance. Because Daniel Bradford was the kind of man who did voices at story time. She hadn't known that about him. But there was a lot she hadn't known about him.

Daniel gave a weary shrug—one Chloe didn't buy in the slightest—and headed upstairs. Kelly went to one of the kitchen cabinets, pulled out some wine glasses, filled them with Chardonnay from the fridge and plopped one down in front of Chloe.

'Really, I shouldn't...'

Kelly just nudged the glass closer.

Chloe picked it up and took a tiny sip. She'd accused Daniel of only seeing what he'd wanted to see in her. Hadn't she been just as bad? Even though it had been ten years on, he hadn't lost that fantasy edge for her. He'd been that two-dimensional object of a crush, the unattainable alpha man, and she hadn't looked any deeper than he had. She'd been too busy caught up in the fact that the unattainable had suddenly become attainable.

Chloe took a bigger sip.

But now she was seeing the man inside. Not a fantasy. Not a dream. Just a wounded man who was trying to deal with the bullets life had shot through his heart. And, damn, if that didn't mean she was starting to fall for him.

She took a whacking great gulp of wine.

'How's things?' Kelly said, eyeing her up and down.

Chloe slumped forward and let her forehead hit the table.

'That good, huh?'

Her brow squeaked against the varnished wood as she nodded. Kelly just went and got the bottle out of the fridge and placed it on the table between them.

'What's my brother done now?' she asked.

Chloe sat up and shook her head, pursing her lips. Where on earth should she start?

'He likes you, you know.'

Chloe didn't say anything. That was what she was afraid of. It was much easier when he was hating her, pitying her. There was no chance of hoping then. She decided to take another tack.

'He told me about his wife and son,' she said quietly.

Kelly nodded and took a long swig of her wine. 'Pretty much destroyed him,' she said. 'He loved that boy so much...'

She trailed off and her focus became distant. It was a while before she could speak again. It was a while before Chloe was ready for her to.

'And he worshipped Paula. But they couldn't put what they'd had back together after Joshua died. She retreated into a world of bitterness and guilt and he didn't know how to follow.' Kelly looked at Chloe. 'She hated him for that.'

She reached over and covered Chloe's hand with hers. 'He's just really scared, you know? It's not that he doesn't know how to love, but that when he does it's so full-on...' She shook her head. 'He can't stand the thought of loving and losing again, so he just doesn't let himself care. Be patient with him.'

Chloe wanted to pull her hand away, but she thought it might offend her friend. 'Oh, I'm not sure if...' If what?

If she wanted him to care? She wanted it so badly it hurt. Didn't mean it was going to happen.

'Is that what happened with Georgia?' she asked.

Kelly frowned and stared into her glass of wine for a moment. 'Maybe. I don't know. On paper they should have been perfect for each other. I really love Georgia, really hoped she'd be able to get him to unlock, but for a long time they just drifted along and then I think she pushed him too hard, too fast.'

Chloe nodded, and then she asked the question she really didn't want the answer to. 'Do you think he'll ever be ready?'

Kelly stared at her, a pained expression on her face. 'I don't know…I want him to be, and I thought he was getting better, but me being ill brought it all up again. He seemed to shut down further. I think I scared the hell out of him.'

Chloe smiled softly. 'He loves you. Anyone can see that.'

One corner of Kelly's mouth curled. 'Well, I am pretty lovable.'

There was a noise on the stairs—Daniel's heavy tread—and Chloe gathered the rest of her belongings together and put them in her bag. She stood up and smiled first at Kelly and then at Daniel as he entered the room.

'I'd better be going,' she said. 'It's been a long day.'

Before she had any more wine. Before she let it encourage her to do something stupid—like believing she could mend Daniel Bradford if she wanted to badly enough.

ELEVEN

—

It was a bright, crisp Saturday afternoon. Chloe and Daniel met in her living room, more out of choice than necessity. It was Ben's third birthday and Daniel's house was undergoing a mutiny at the hands of a gang of knee-high pirates.

It felt like returning to the scene of a crime, even though it was her own space. She'd managed to block the memories out while she'd been on her own, but when Daniel rapped on the big glass door at the end of her living room, it all came flooding back. Thank goodness for the steely winter light seeping into every corner, making everything seem bleak and grey. She didn't think she could have stood it if it had been like that night— humid and warm and intimate.

They sat at her dining table, Chloe filling in the huge master plan she'd sketched out while Daniel pointed and made suggestions.

'I've had an idea for that arch we're going to have over the pool,' she told him. 'I know we said colourful, but I wondered if, rather than an explosion of shades, we did something more structured?'

Daniel stopped scribbling on a scrap of paper in his scratchy handwriting. 'Like?'

'I'm thinking the arch could be a spectrum of colours, like a rainbow.'

Daniel screwed up his face. 'Stripes? I don't think we've got enough room.'

She shook her head gently. 'No...not so literal. I was thinking more of a gradual colour change, starting with reds and oranges at one end of the arch and subtly merging all the way through the different shades until we get to purples and violets at the other.' She pulled her notebook out and showed him a sketch she'd done the night before. 'Like this...with ferns and pitchers and palm leaves all interspersed throughout.' And she made a few deft pencil lines on the drawing to show him what she meant.

He picked the pad up and stared at it, and then he looked at her.

It was that expression again. The one that made her want to throw 'calm and professional' out of the window and drown it in the river. She pushed her chair back and headed for her kitchenette.

'I want a coffee. Do you want a coffee?' And then she busied herself filling the kettle so she didn't have to wait for his answer.

She heard him cross the carpet to meet her, but she kept on fussing with sugar pots and instant coffee jars all the same.

'Chloe?' His voice was soft as velvet.

'I'll be right with you in a minute,' she said brightly,

and noticed her hand was shaking as she tried to pour boiling water into the mugs.

Daniel came up behind her, took the kettle out of her hand and placed it back on its base. Then he put a hand on each shoulder and turned her to face him. 'I think the arch idea is very much like the woman who created it.'

Chloe swallowed. Naive? Out of step? Been there, done that before?

He smiled a little as he read the emotions flitting over her face. 'I think it's inspired,' he said. 'Complicated. Unique.'

Oh, hell, thought Chloe.

Then he leaned towards her and brushed his lips against hers. She froze for a moment, before kissing him back then pulling away. 'This isn't a good idea.'

'Why not?'

She stepped away and folded her arms across her middle to keep them from doing anything stupid. 'Because, one day, I will want a husband and a family and you don't want those things.'

'One day isn't today, Chloe. Can't we just have now? You know this is more than just a fling.'

She did know. She just wasn't sure what to do with that knowledge.

'Maybe I'll want those things too,' he said. 'One day.'

One day... He'd spoken so softly, but he still hadn't been able to hide his tension as he'd said those words, as if he secretly preferred it was the kind of tomorrow that was always one day out of reach.

She looked at him. Maybe wasn't good enough. She couldn't live with *maybe* from Daniel. He'd rejected her twice already and she wasn't prepared to risk it again.

The last time they'd been in this room had been bad enough, but really he'd just been rejecting New Chloe. Fake Chloe, as she'd now started to refer to her alter ego. The shell she'd built to protect herself from the likes of Daniel Bradford.

He'd actually done her a favour. While it hadn't felt good, that shell had needed to be broken. It had become so thick that she was isolating herself from everyone behind a wall of supposed perfection. New Chloe had deserved to be smashed to smithereens.

However, what had emerged in her place wasn't the Mouse. It was someone new. A Chloe cocktail—a mix of the best of both with a little something extra thrown in for good measure. This fledgling Chloe had some of the confidence and maturity of the new, tempered with the approachability and warmth of the old. A little of her impulsiveness too—but not so much to make her want to press the self-destruct button again.

But this new creature was delicate. Only just formed, with skin like paper. Daniel wasn't ready for this Chloe. And she couldn't wait another ten years for him to be ready. She needed to get on with her life, start living it for herself instead of what everyone else expected for her.

'I can't get involved with you, Daniel. I like you too much.'

He looked at her as if she'd lost her senses. 'What kind of bizarre female logic is that?'

Chloe's expression hardened. 'The kind that's going to save us both a whole lot of grief.'

'You're wrong,' he said. 'I'm not that same man who ran a mile from an unexpected proposal last year. I've changed. Come out with me on a proper date.' He gave her that smile he knew she couldn't resist, the rotter. 'We never did try that Italian...'

She walked out of the double doors that led out onto a small deck with a table and chairs and a variety of terracotta planters filled with ivy and heather and miniature evergreens. Daniel followed her. She leaned on the rail and looked over the greyish-green glossy water that glinted in the winter sun.

'We've been on this merry-go-round before. It's not the dates—or the lack of them—that's the problem.' She twisted her head to look at him. 'We just always seem to do it for the wrong reason, and I'm not sure this time's any different.'

'Don't say that.' He stepped in close behind her, folded his arms around her front and buried his face in the hollow of her neck. It was all Chloe could do not to melt against him.

'I can't be your experiment,' she told him in a whisper, 'to see if you're ready for more than a fling.'

'Why not? Isn't life about taking chances, exploring new possibilities? Think of the plants we work with. We wouldn't even know of their existence if everyone decided to stay home and never go into unexplored territory.'

She slid out of his grasp and walked to the opposite corner of the deck. 'But some risks are too costly. I know you know what I'm talking about.'

The smile slid from his face.

'There are places inside us that can hurt so badly that we never want to go back there,' she said, knowing he understood every syllable, that his mind had wandered to his devastated marriage and the little boy he'd never got to watch grow up. 'And you're not the only one who has them.'

His gaze grew intense.

She inhaled and let the air out slowly, gathering her courage. 'Last time we were together here—'

'I explained about that…apologised…'

She nodded. She knew he had, but he needed to understand.

'What you said hurt,' she replied firmly, catching his eye and keeping his focus locked on her. 'But, really, it wasn't anything more than wounded pride. You didn't even know me then, not really, because I was being so good at being Miss Fancy Knickers—yes, I know what they used to call me—that I didn't even know myself.'

She let out a little laugh that died quickly.

'This is it, now…' She held her arms out wide. 'This is me. It's different. I *feel* different. And you know who Chloe is now. Not a geeky student with a crush. Not a vamp with perfect nail polish. Just a girl who likes orchids and happens to possess a killer shoe collection.'

'Of course it's different. That's why it could work this time.'

Could. That sounded an awful lot like *maybe* to her.

'Call me a coward, but I can't take that chance. If you did it again—if you pushed me away one more time—it'd kill me.'

'But I won't!'

'You're saying you won't ever push me away? I thought you didn't *do* for ever any more.'

Daniel stuttered, and she knew he'd just reacted to her words without thinking them through.

'We both know you're not in the market for that. If it's not going to end in wedding rings and honeymoons then, one day, someone will leave, and I have the feeling it would be you.'

'Why? Why would it be me?'

He just kept coming, didn't he? Batting away her arguments one by one, because that was his way: he set his mind to a goal and he pursued it relentlessly, no matter what. But he'd set his heart on the wrong goal this time. She wasn't something to be won; she was something to be treasured. Kept. And he just couldn't promise her that. So she stepped forward, looked him straight in the eye and said the one thing she knew would scare him away for good.

'Because I'm falling in love with you,' she said simply, and watched the colour drain from his face as her words hit home. She'd known it would happen, but it hadn't made it any easier to watch.

'I...I...'

'Please!' She held up a palm. 'Don't try to say it back. You'd be insulting both of us.'

He closed his mouth and it became a grim line.

She walked back into the living room. 'You can go now.'

'Chloe...'

'I know you want to,' she said. 'I can see it in your eyes.'

He didn't deny it, damn him. He didn't deny it.

She pulled herself up straight, put her best professional face on. 'No need for any more meetings. Next week we'll be revealing the plans to our team and starting work. We've done as much as we can do, you and I.

"Calm and professional"—that was what we said, didn't we?' She stopped and looked at her shoes. 'Maybe we should have just stuck to that.'

And then she turned and walked back indoors, because she couldn't watch him leave. Not one more time.

Daniel hated himself for walking away from Chloe's houseboat. But he'd had that sudden reality check that only one fly in ten got when it was hovering above one of his plants. The future promised to be bright and sweet and full of everything he secretly wanted, but he knew that once he gave into that feeling, once he climbed down inside it and let go, there would be no going back, even if he realised it had been a terrible mistake.

He tried to make up for it in little ways over the following weeks. One morning he brought her a cup of her favourite coffee and put it in her nursery just minutes before she arrived for work. Another day he left a copy of an article he'd seen in a magazine that she'd find interesting. Chloe didn't say anything about it at all. In fact, she seemed to have gone back to being that strange robot she'd been after that unfortunate night in the summer. But she seemed to manage to smile and laugh and talk with the other staff as they prepared for the Beauty and the Beast Festival.

He knew he couldn't give her what she really wanted, but that didn't mean they couldn't be friends, right? He missed her. Missed hearing her laugh, or seeing her deep in conversation about something she was excited about, her hands moving rapidly as she spoke with both body and voice.

They had to work together for the next couple of

weeks and he'd much prefer they left it on a good footing. Then he could leave on the expedition to Borneo knowing he'd done as much as he could, and he'd be free, no longer weighed down by the guilt that had been steadily solidifying in him since he'd seen that hurt look in her eyes.

So, at the end of the working day, as everyone was packing up, preparing to go home, he made his way to her part of the nursery.

'Hi,' he said as he walked in the door.

She looked up from what she was doing. 'Hi.' And then she just stared at him.

He held out a square object wrapped in a supermarket carrier bag. A peace offering. Not one for gift-wrapping, was Daniel.

Her features pinched together, but she took it from him. The rustling of the thin plastic seemed unnaturally loud in the deserted greenhouse. She pulled the square object out and looked at it. For a long time she was very still, and then, just moving her eyes and leaving her head bowed, she looked at him. 'What is this?'

'It's a print of the slipper orchid from my book. I thought you'd like it.'

She stared back at the picture. What? Was it out of focus? Had he put it in backwards?

'Is there something wrong?' he asked, not liking the frown that was bunching up her forehead.

She took a step forward. 'Yes, there is. I want you to stop being nice to me.'

'I beg your pardon?'

'It's just making it all that much harder,' she said.

'I was just trying to…I don't know…apologise.'

'What for?' She folded her arms across her chest. 'For not being in love with me? As much as I love a good moccachino or a pretty picture, even I don't think they're quite going to cover that one.'

When she put it like that, maybe...

'I wasn't trying to upset you,' he said. 'But I leave on the fifteenth of next month. I just didn't want things to be weird between us up until then.'

The frown melted and her features sagged. 'The fifteenth? That's the day after the festival.'

'I know.'

She nodded, looked away. 'Okay. Maybe that's a good thing.' The way her jaw was clamped together made him believe otherwise. She met his gaze again. 'So we just have to last another three weeks and then you'll be gone.'

Last another three weeks? That sounded very ominous. Very final.

'I'm not going for good,' he reminded her.

'For long enough, though,' she replied. 'Almost two months.'

He nodded, and he realised that the thought of the trip no longer filled him with the same restless energy that he'd experienced when he'd set it all up. Somehow, it felt like running away, even though it seemed Chloe was quite keen for him to put on his shoes and sprint.

He hadn't wanted it to end like this. Awkward. Sad.

'Is bringing you a coffee now and then really that bad?' he asked.

'Yes,' she said and her eyes began to shimmer.

He walked towards her but she held up a hand. 'Don't... Please...'

'But—'

She shook her head and suddenly that shimmer in her eyes turned to anger.

'I know you're not meaning to, but you're just playing games with me. It's the whole "want what you can't have" thing. You can't help yourself.'

That wasn't it at all. He opened his mouth to tell her as much, but she cut in before the words had left his mouth.

'It's got to stop, Daniel! You're not being fair. Please...' That little waver in her voice, right there, got him right down in his gut. Her lip wobbled and the next word was barely a whisper. '*Please*, just leave me alone.'

And then she turned and walked out of the door, leaving the framed print on the bench.

When Daniel got home he found his sister waiting for him. She met him at the kitchen door with a bottle of chilled champagne in her hand.

He really didn't feel like celebrating. 'What's this in aid of?' he asked her.

Kelly nodded to an open manila envelope on the kitchen table. 'Papers arrived. As of today, I am officially divorced.' She waved the bottle at him. 'But I didn't want to drink this on my own, because that would just be...you know...sad.' And then she grinned at him, just to prove how elated she was.

Daniel walked over to her, took the bottle out of her hand, placed it on the table and pulled her into a fierce hug.

After a moment, she pushed herself away, exhaling hard. 'Just don't be too nice to me, okay?'

Daniel threw his hands in the air in mock surrender. What was wrong with the womankind today? Seriously?

He opened the champagne while Kelly got two flutes from the cupboard and when their glasses were filled they both went to sit on the sofa at the end of the conservatory.

'So, how does it feel to be finally free?' he asked, slightly elated himself that her rat of an ex-husband was out of his life also. Kelly had moaned long and hard about the process of eradicating that scum from her life.

'Bloody terrible,' she said and downed almost the whole glass in one go.

'But—'

'Oh, I don't want him back,' she added quickly. 'But it's hard, you know.' She glanced at the kitchen ceiling, which also happened to be the underside of Cal's bedroom. 'Hard on the boys and hard to feel so...alone.'

He nodded. He'd felt that way once, but then he'd become so used to it he hadn't been able to remember a time when it was easier not to be that way. And now? Now he just wanted...

Chloe.

He wanted to be with Chloe.

But she didn't want to be with him—and he had to admit she might have some very good reasons for that. He sighed.

Kelly slugged back the last of her champagne. 'Oh, and I ought to tell you that I think the boys and I should move out when you get back from the jungle. Late April, maybe.'

He sat up, almost snorted bubbles out of his left nostril. 'What?' he half said, half coughed.

Kelly gave him a rueful smile. 'It's not that the boys and I don't love living here,' she said, 'but it's time I stood on my own two feet, faced the world.'

'Kells, you don't have to! Think of the money...!'

She laid a firm hand on his arm. 'I know. But I need to do this. For me.'

He shrugged. Kelly had made up her mind. And when a Bradford made up their mind there was no budging them.

'Then I'll help any way I can,' he said.

That was when his sister burst into tears.

She crawled up to him, buried her head in his shoulder and sobbed until there was no more moisture left in her body, it seemed. Daniel didn't quite know what to do. If she were a plant he'd stand her in a bucket of water to rehydrate her, but if there was one thing he'd learnt this year it was that people were a heck of a lot more complicated than plants.

She peeled herself from him, blew her nose and went to refill her glass from the bottle on the table. As she crossed the room she fixed him with those beady eyes of hers.

'So...' she said as she sat down '...we know all about me, but what's got *you* looking as joyful as a turkey at Christmas?'

He aimed for humour and ended up with *disgruntled*. 'Chloe thinks I'm stalking her.'

Kelly threw back her head and laughed. When she'd finished wiping a fresh batch of tears from her eyes she said, 'Thanks, I needed that.'

'Your sympathy is duly noted and appreciated.'

Kelly just grinned at him. 'Why does she think that?'

'It's stupid,' he said, and he was just about to tell her how stupid when he could hear his own voice in his head, laying out his case. But instead he started to think about all those women who'd turned up at Kew just to see him. Had they not been able to think about anything else for more than five minutes at a time? Had they had the same urge to get as close to him as possible, for as long as they could? Was this what obsession felt like?

Oh, hell. It was, wasn't it?

Maybe he needed psychiatric help.

'Oh, I've been saying that for years,' his sister said over the top of her champagne glass.

Daniel glared at her. Had he actually said that out loud? Things were worse than he thought.

And then she reached over and ruffled his hair. 'It needs a cut,' she said as she put her glass down and stood up. 'And I need some shut-eye.'

She walked over to the table, retrieved the bottle and topped his glass up. 'And, for what it's worth, I don't think you're crazy. In fact, this is the most sensible I've seen you in years.'

She dumped her empty glass in the dishwasher. 'If you like, Dr Kelly will give you her diagnosis.'

Daniel made a face that said she'd better not try, but as Kelly walked across the room and kissed him on the cheek she whispered in his ear, 'I'd say the problem is this—you've got it bad.'

TWELVE

'Daniel?' It was Kelly's voice on the other end of the line, but not her usual sarcastic drawl. His little sister sounded really panicked.

It was the first day of the orchid festival, and Daniel and Chloe and the whole team had arrived early and were working hard to make all the finishing touches before the grand opening later that morning. The Princess of Wales Conservatory was looking amazing, dripping with colour and unusual displays. Next to the otherworldly shapes of some of the pitchers and other carnivores, the orchids only seemed more delicate and fragile.

Daniel ducked into the Temperate Carnivores section, letting the door close behind him, cutting off the noise of the work party. 'What is it?'

'It's Ben,' she whimpered. 'He fell off the climbing frame at pre-school and cracked his head.' There was a pause while she took a great, snuffling breath. 'We're in the hospital. He's unconscious, Dan.'

Daniel didn't waste any time joining his sister in panicking. He got the name of the A&E department they were in, explained the situation to the nearest person with a Kew T-shirt and sprinted off in the direction of the staff car park. Within fifteen minutes he was at the hospital, haranguing the young guy on Reception into telling him where his sister and nephew were.

He found Kelly, sitting quietly and composed in a cubicle, with her son drowsy on the trolley beside her. Her body was rigid, her knees clamped together and her knuckles white as she gripped onto herself for comfort.

'He came round,' she said in a tight voice. 'The doctor says that's a good sign, but they did scans and they want to keep him in for observation.'

Daniel just walked over to his sister and pulled her up out of the chair and into his arms. He was angry. Really angry. Angry this had happened to Ben. Angry Kelly had to face something like this all on her own. Angry at Ben's father...just *because*. And he decided he'd like to stay angry, because angry was a lot better than *scared witless*.

'You're cutting off my air supply,' Kelly said hoarsely and poked him in the ribs.

'Sorry,' he said, standing her back from him and holding her at arm's length, his hands on her shoulders. He looked her up and down. 'Are you okay?'

'I am now,' she said, and he saw a hint of the old Kelly in her thin smile. She was a fighter, his sister. The strongest person he knew.

He walked over to Ben's trolley. The little boy's eyelids were fluttering and he hauled them open. 'Uncle Daniel,' he said, and his chubby fingers made a grasping motion. Daniel stuck his index finger in Ben's palm, as he had done when Ben had been a baby, and the boy grabbed onto it tightly. His lids drifted closed.

He couldn't go anywhere now without disturbing his nephew. A throb of panic set itself inside Daniel's temple. He wasn't sure if he could do this. Even though he hadn't been there when Joshua had—

He couldn't finish that thought.

Even though he hadn't been there, something about seeing this tiny body curled up on the pristine white of a hospital sheet was bringing all those feelings flooding back. He glanced at the gap in the cubicle curtain. The urge to dart through it was overpowering, but with Ben holding tightly onto his finger he was trapped.

He looked at Ben, his almost-translucent lids closed and his mouth relaxed into an 'o' shape, and something inside Daniel's chest cramped. Since Kelly had moved in, he'd really let himself get attached to his nephews. He wanted to scold himself for being reckless, but how could he? That was what families were supposed to do— care about each other. That was what people were supposed to do in general.

But if Daniel tried to count on one hand the number of people that he'd truly let himself care about since the end of his marriage, he realised he still had a couple of fingers left. Even Kelly and the boys had to worm their way in slowly. What kind of brother did that make him?

What kind of man did that make him?

Kelly came to stand by the trolley and rhythmically smoothed her son's hair from his forehead, then she reached out and circled Daniel's other thumb with her smaller hand, mirroring her son's gesture, and the three of them stayed like that in silence for a moment, joined like a circle.

'This,' he said croakily, 'is why I can't do it again.'

She nodded and a tear dripped from the corner of one eye. She couldn't wipe it away without breaking contact, so she let it run down her cheek, the overhang of her jaw and onto her neck.

'I get that, Dan,' she said softly—far too softly for his ballsy little sister. 'But tell me this: would you rather have had those six months with Joshua or would you rather that he hadn't existed at all?'

Daniel flinched at the mention of his son's name. He realised he hadn't said it out loud for years. It was just as well it wasn't him hooked up to one of those heart monitors, because the little cubicle would've been filled with the sound of a galloping electronic horse.

Thankfully, he was rescued from answering Kelly's question by the arrival of a doctor. He prised his finger from Ben's hand, shot a quick look at Kelly, then went to wait outside while the doctor delivered her news.

Kelly opened her mouth and reached a hand in his direction, and he knew she was going to say it was fine for him to stay, but he needed to get out of there. If it was going to be bad news, he didn't know if he could take it.

Inside, deep down in his core, he was shaking and cold. And as he searched for a free plastic chair to perch on his conscience began to nibble away at him too, adding a dash of nausea to the already uncomfortable internal cocktail.

He glanced at Ben's pale blue cubicle curtain, knowing that inside Kelly was probably feeling worse than he was, that he'd left her there alone to deal with whatever was coming.

He'd told himself that he was brave because he liked climbing high walls and tramped through rain forests and knew how to deal with leeches and ticks, but this was where it counted. Here. In this drab city hospital. This was where he would prove he was a man or not.

Brave? Don't make him laugh.

So Daniel paused for a moment, rubbed his face with both hands, then he marched back over to the curtain, pulled it aside and went to join his sister.

That evening, after Ben had been discharged from the hospital, the doctors assuring his mother he'd be fine, Daniel travelled halfway across London to go climbing. Even though this centre had a wall thirty feet taller than the one at his local climbing place, it still wasn't high enough.

Never mind, a sarcastic little voice in his head said. *You'll be in reach of a real mountain in a week's time. You'll be happy then.*

He grabbed for another handhold, pulled himself up and searched for the next place to put his foot. Maybe this wall wasn't tall enough, but he could climb it more than once, couldn't he?

But now there was a second voice inside his head. Most annoyingly, it belonged to his sister. And he realised he'd been doing a pretty good job of ignoring it since the night they'd toasted her divorce papers.

He decided he was under the wrong bit of the overhang to make his way past it, so he backtracked a bit and chose another route. As he groped sideways for a handhold he noticed a lean, dark-haired guy about his own age looking at him, studying him.

Daniel scowled at him briefly before continuing his climb. What was his problem?

As he climbed he considered the question Kelly had posed to him in the hospital. Would he, given the chance, erase his wife and son from his life completely, make it as if they had never existed? Would he choose freedom over pain?

He cracked the door of his memory open and saw Josh's gummy smile, how his face had lit up every time Daniel had come home from work. He remembered how his son had smelled after a bath, and how, as a newborn, he'd clung monkey-like to his shoulder as Daniel had paced and sung to him in the small hours of the night.

Would he want to erase those memories if he could? Maybe he would. He'd tried his hardest to pretend they weren't there for so long.

But when he tried to stuff the images he'd let loose away, they refused to go. Instead, they settled them-selves into a corner of his consciousness, and when he let his mind wander in that direction he found, not nec-essarily joy, but warmth. Comfort. Not the screaming six-headed black dragon he'd expected to find. It seemed odd he'd run from them for so long.

Daniel stopped where he was on the wall, arrested by that thought. A couple of other climbers had to work their way round him while he hung there.

Running.

Not like a hunter chasing something, but like some-thing being hunted. Had he really, all these years, had it all back to front?

And running from what? What was it that terrified him? He took a deep breath and mentally turned round to face it.

Love.

That was what it was. In any shape or any form. He'd even run from his family until circumstances had caused him to let Kelly and her boys into his life. But that was understandable, because love wasn't a pretty thing full of hearts and flowers and rose petals. No, love *was* the six-headed monster, viciously devouring everything in its path, mincing it up and spitting it out to bleed.

He almost closed his eyes to block out the image, but then those memories that had been sitting quietly in the corner tapped him on the shoulder. They replayed themselves for him, and then they introduced him to a few more.

Daniel hauled in a shuddering breath.

Just like plants, human beings needed certain things to thrive. Oh, it would be so easy if those things were just light and water and good manure. So easy. But, no, humans needed more complicated things. Things like closeness and connection. Otherwise they could be healthy specimens on the outside, but they'd be dried up and withered inside. Human beings needed love.

He started climbing again, more slowly this time. He'd always be hunted by it until the last of his days. And he was so tired of running. He didn't want to do it any more. It didn't bring peace. It didn't bring safety. All it brought was the promise that the next day would be another sprint. And the next. And the next...

And, really, there was no point in him running anyway. He was already in that trap, with no escape. Just like the fly that stupidly buzzed and exhausted itself trying to get out of the pitcher he was exhausting himself for nothing.

There was no point in struggling. It only made things worse.

He thought about Kelly, how she'd smoothed Ben's hair in the hospital, a look of fierce determination on her face. She didn't run. She chose to stay and fight, no matter what. Over the last couple of years she'd shown a strength and courage that put him to shame.

And that knowledge stirred something inside him.

They were made of the same stuff, him and Kelly. And, maybe, just maybe, if she could do this, so could he.

Oh, how Chloe hated Valentine's Day.

It seemed the whole twenty-four hours had decided to gang up and make a mockery of her. Not only was it the last day of the orchid festival—the one packed with all the PR events, meaning she was forced to stay close to Daniel—but in the back of her head was a clock, counting down to the following morning, when he would leave.

It was torture.

If only…a little part of her kept saying. If only he was ready… If only he felt the same way about you that you feel about him…

A camera flash went off, hitting the back of her eyeballs with searing force. She blinked and tried to maintain the smile the PR woman had insisted they paste on, all the while trying to ignore the prickling of her skin because he was near.

She was worrying herself. Mainly because she was having recurrent fantasies where she invited him back to her houseboat for one last hot night before he disappeared from her life. Possibly for good.

It was a bad, bad idea.

Because she'd fallen in love with him anyway. And, if she felt as if something were ripping her insides out piece by piece now, what would it be like if she truly removed every last barrier and gave herself completely to him? She had to hang onto something, some piece of herself she wouldn't lose. And, while she mourned Daniel's inability to let himself love anything or anyone, she totally, totally understood it. If only she could achieve that nirvana of numbness herself.

She was standing beside him at the edge of the lily pad pool, in front of the brightly coloured rainbow of flowers she'd designed, but shortly everyone would move along to the Nash Conservatory, another of Kew's old glasshouses, where the auction itself would be held. 'That's all for now,' the photographer yelled as she checked her display, and Chloe started to leave. She saw Daniel move towards her, but after a second of eye contact that made her almost dizzy holding everything she was feeling back, she looked away, allowed herself to be bustled along to the next event. As much as she didn't want to see him go, she was pretty sure she would fall apart completely if she had to talk to him.

As she'd said—torture.

The rest of the afternoon went in a bit of a blur. Before she knew it the sun was low in the sky, painting gold squares through the windows onto the wall of the Nash Conservatory, and she was sitting on a low platform near the auctioneer's lectern with a few other select members of the team, ready to give a brief description of each specimen on sale that night. At least Daniel was at the other end of the row, giving her a vague chance of breathing.

However, the fact she knew he was looking at her, even though she refused to meet his gaze, was counteracting that completely.

The place was packed. Full of orchid and carnivorous plant enthusiasts as well as fervent Kew supporters, the general public and quite a few reporters and TV cameras. More than once she saw them zoom in on Daniel, who was looking wonderfully gruff and brooding with his arms crossed over his front as he slouched in his chair.

She closed her eyes and sent up a silent prayer.

Please...please, let her get through this without making a total fool of herself. That was all she asked.

Daniel was definitely *not* in the mood to smile for the cameras, even if the Channel Six woman batted her lashes at him so hard she started a typhoon. All day long he'd been trying to talk to Chloe, and all day long he'd failed. Partly because of the flurry of activity it took to pull an event like this together, but partly because he sensed she was keeping her distance. It was driving him bananas.

He needed to talk to her—face to face, one to one— and now it looked as if he might be robbed of that chance entirely he wasn't inclined to look very happy. And Daniel was not good at pretending to be happy when he wasn't.

He saw a camera pointed in his direction, a zoom

lens being focused, and he just scowled harder. He had things he needed to discuss with Chloe—plans—and it couldn't wait until tomorrow. In just over twelve hours he'd be at the airport.

The auctioneer banged his gavel and Daniel jumped. One of Chloe's lots was up first. She walked past him and a waft of her perfume hit his nostrils. She began to talk about the Miltonia hybrid in her husky voice and he felt as if he wanted to climb out of his skin. He'd wanted to hear that voice all afternoon, but not giving facts and growing instructions; he wanted to hear her saying his name.

It seemed as if a thousand lots passed before his eyes, as if they'd sold off the entire contents of all the glass-houses and the arboretum, but really the whole auction must have lasted less than two hours.

Even then there was no let-up. The PR team wouldn't set them free, insisting on more photos and, to top it all, a live TV interview for the evening news. The team was directed back onto the stage in front of some of the larger orchid displays that had been transported from the Princess of Wales Conservatory to be used as a backdrop.

Someone from the news crew rearranged the inter-viewees and he ended up standing next to Chloe. He caught her eye and she held his gaze for just a moment, but it was long enough. Long enough to know she was finding this just as unbearable as he was. He'd find a way to talk to her somehow, he would. They just needed to get through this interview first.

The reporter turned to the camera, smiled, and started her spiel. 'This is Melissa Morgan for Channel

Six news, live at Kew Gardens after their very success-ful tropical plant auction, which has raised thousands of pounds to go towards their conservation work all over the world...'

Daniel tuned her out. He only tuned back in again when he heard her mention first Chloe's name then his own as she introduced them as team leaders for the fes-tival. She looked at Daniel and pointed the microphone too close to his face.

'As Head of Tropical Plants here at Kew, do you feel the festival has been a success?'

'Yes,' he said, then closed his mouth and folded his arms.

She opened her mouth to ask him a question, but he must have been looking particularly uncooperative be-cause at the last moment she swung the microphone in Chloe's direction instead and asked her about the de-sign of the display and what her favourite orchid was.

He snorted gently to himself. It figured. Who'd talk to the Beast when Beauty was at hand?

He could tell Chloe was nervous, however, from the slight waver in her first words, but she was warm and articulate, and he knew the viewing public would be transfixed, just as he was. They would love her.

Just as he did.

But that reporter didn't miss a trick. Too late he saw her notice the way he was looking at Chloe. Too late he looked away, crumpling his features back into his ear-lier scowl.

The reporter let Chloe finish her sentence and then she turned back to Daniel. He didn't miss the slight arch of one eyebrow as she fired off her next question. Guess it hadn't been such a good idea to tick her off.

'This isn't your first Valentine's Day in the spotlight, is it, Daniel?'

If she thought she was getting even one word out of him now she was sadly mistaken. He merely blinked at her, raised his eyebrows in return.

Her eyes narrowed. 'And how is it one year on after your Leap Year proposal?' Her gaze flicked across to Chloe and then back to him. 'Is there any special woman in your life you'd like to give a Valentine's message to?'

Beside him, Chloe stiffened. He saw her glance at the exit.

'I don't think that's any of your business,' he said firmly.

Miss Morgan didn't like that any better than the monosyllable he'd offered her earlier. She narrowed her eyes and turned the microphone back in Chloe's direction.

'And how about you, Chloe? I saw a very interesting picture of you on the Internet a couple of months ago...' She gave Daniel a sideways glance. 'What was it like to finally hook The One That Got Away? Did you decide to throw him back?'

Chloe's mouth moved and she flushed deep pink. He could see the panic in her eyes, knew she was hating every second of this public interrogation.

'You know what?' he said suddenly. 'I would like to answer your question. Maybe it's time I set the record straight, then people might actually get on with their own lives instead of poking their noses into mine.'

'Daniel...' Chloe whispered beside him. 'You don't have to.'

Yes, he did. It was his fault Chloe had been put on the spot like this, and maybe it was time to stop running from this and face it head-on. Maybe it was time to face a lot of things head-on.

'I said no when my girlfriend proposed to me last year,' he began, 'and I don't regret it. What's more, after the success of the Year of Georgia on Radio EROS—' he watched in satisfaction as the reporter frowned at the mention of a rival media company '—I think it's obvious that she's doing much better without me than she was with me. And I can't blame her. I wasn't ready for love or marriage or anything like that then.'

A glint appeared in Melissa Morgan's eyes. He knew what that was—killer instinct. She knew she had a story here and she was going to hunt it down. Luckily for her, Daniel had decided he was going to hand it to her on a plate.

'And you're ready now?' she asked smoothly.

He'd spent weeks trying to let Chloe know how he felt. Unfortunately for him, he hadn't quite realised what those feelings were until it was too late. No wonder she didn't trust him, didn't believe in him. Every time she'd put herself on the line for him, he'd pulled back. Well, now it was his turn, and he wasn't going to run away from it.

He let the scowl melt from his features, looked the reporter in the eye and began to talk. 'Turning Georgia down was the best thing I ever did—for me and for her. Without that, I wouldn't have had the spotlight turned on me, and, in turn, I wouldn't have had to take a good, hard look at myself.'

Beside him, Chloe started to fidget. He stopped looking at the reporter and looked at her instead. She met his gaze, and he could see hope and fear and sadness and discomfort warring behind her eyes. 'This year I met someone,' he said softly.

Morgan nudged the microphone closer and he resisted the urge to bat it away. She needed to hear this. Everyone needed to hear this, especially Chloe.

'I met a woman,' he continued. 'An amazing, brave woman, who showed me what it really meant to be fearless, who showed me what courage—what dignity— looked like…and I fell completely and hopelessly in love with her.'

Chloe's eyes began to shimmer. She shook her head gently, her hand pressed against her breastbone.

'Yes,' he said, starting to smile, willing her to join him. 'I love you, Chloe.'

And then he shoved the microphone out of the way, stepped forward and kissed her. The room, which had descended into a thick silence as soon as he'd begun to talk, suddenly erupted into cheers and applause. There was a gentle tapping on his shoulder, but he ignored it, because Chloe was kissing him back, kissing him so softly and sweetly that he finally had no doubt that she felt the same way.

But the tapping continued and he dragged himself away from Chloe's lips. 'What?' he said gruffly. 'Can't you see I'm busy?'

That earned him a laugh. Even Chloe chuckled. He was funny. Who knew?

Melissa Morgan was grinning at him, but her grin had an edge of something else in it too. 'I can see that,' she said, laughing softly, but Daniel was close enough to see the calculating glint in her eye. 'But I thought I might repeat my earlier question...'

She looked between Chloe and Daniel, blinked slowly, and then positioned the microphone in Daniel's direction. 'So...*is* there a Valentine's message you'd like to deliver?'

The meaning behind her words hit him like a lightning bolt. He knew what she was asking, what she was pushing for...the Valentine's story to top all other Valentine's stories this year. And he also knew it was the one way he could convince Chloe he was serious about this, serious about her...

He made a nod so minuscule that only the reporter saw it. One corner of her mouth hiked up in a knowing smile, and she stepped back a little, still holding the microphone out.

Daniel swallowed. Nerves hit him in a wave of nausea, but he knew he had to do this, knew now that he wanted it more than anything. Maybe that was why he'd been running so hard in the other direction all year.

It was now or never. The six-headed monster needed to be slain once and for all, and hadn't he always said he was the hunter, not the prey?

He took Chloe's fingers, lifted them in his own and covered them with his other hand, then he slid one foot back and let both knees bend, one up in front of the other. The crowd around them gasped.

He looked into Chloe's face and realised he couldn't tell what she was thinking. A moment ago, she'd been smiling blissfully, but now her features had frozen and she was blinking rapidly.

He took a deep breath. 'I love you,' he said again, and saw her nod, just slightly, and he knew she believed him. That made the next bit a little easier. 'I know I'm the biggest idiot in the universe...' he saw a glimmer of something in her eyes that just might have been humour and that spurred him on '...and I don't deserve another chance, but I can't go without proving how serious I am.' He took in a deep breath. 'Chloe Michaels, will you marry me?'

Chloe stared at Daniel. She thought her heart might have stopped beating. Her brain had certainly stopped working. She could feel her pulse throbbing in the hand he was holding. It rushed and pumped, filling the silence, filling every part of her.

She couldn't doubt the sincerity in his eyes. He'd meant what he'd said, yet...

Yet...

A couple of weeks ago he hadn't even been able to say how he felt about her. She knew he had baggage. *Lots* of baggage. Was this really the right time? And, if he hadn't been going overseas tomorrow, if he hadn't been pushed into it by that witch of a TV reporter, would he have asked her today? Would he have asked her at all?

The room had been perfectly still for far too many seconds, but that immaculate silence now broke. People began to move. Somebody coughed. She glanced over her shoulder at the gathered crowd. Every single face was turned towards her. Every pair of eyes was heavy on her.

She looked back at Daniel.

She wanted to believe him, really wanted to...but he'd

backed off too many times before. When would be the next time? At the altar? She couldn't let it go that far. She had to be certain.

She opened her mouth, and Daniel pulled her hand towards his lips and then he closed his eyes and kissed it tenderly. A tear slipped down Chloe's cheek.

All of her. He'd said he'd loved all of her.

And heaven knew he'd seen the worst of her—the bits no one else had a clue existed.

He opened his eyes and looked at her again. The proof of his feelings was there for anyone to see. Intensity, yes, but softness too, and a tenderness she'd never seen before.

Chloe swallowed. She knew.

She knew what her answer had to be.

She moistened her lips with the tip of her tongue, and every single backside in that room shifted forward on its seat. She looked into Daniel's eyes, let him know how real her love was for him before she formed the words with her mouth.

Her voice rang out clear, even though she was sure it was going to catch on the barbs in her throat. 'I'm sorry,' she said, shaking her head. 'No. I can't marry you, Daniel.'

The room around them went wild.

THIRTEEN

———

Chloe shivered as she stood on Daniel's porch. At this time of year, dawn was still an hour or so away. Was it too early to knock? She had no idea what time Kelly and the boys got up and she didn't want to disturb them. But she also didn't know what time Daniel's flight was—apart from this morning—and she had to see him before he left.

She checked her watch again. Five fifty-six. She watched the second hand sweep round. When it hit twelve again she screwed up her face, grabbed for the door knocker and rapped twice. It sounded like gunshots in the silent street.

For the longest time there was no light, no movement at all, but then she saw a patch of dull orange through the obscured glass of the Victorian door. And then she heard thudding on the stairs. Moments later the door opened and she was face to face with a crumpled-looking Kelly, a fluffy pink dressing gown clutched around her and held tight with the hand that wasn't on the door. When she saw Chloe her expression changed from one of sleepy befuddlement to something entirely less welcoming.

'For heaven's sake, Chloe! Have you gone *completely* insane?'

Chloe wet her lips with her tongue. She considered nodding, but instead she said, 'Can I see him?' Her breath came out in shaky white puffs on the predawn air.

Kelly's brow lowered further. 'Too late. He's already gone.'

Chloe hadn't been prepared for the cold stab to her stomach at that news. 'No…' she murmured, feeling a violent stinging in the bridge of her nose.

Kelly stared at her, and then she said, 'Oh, for crying out loud! Come in. I need to talk to you.'

She hesitated for a second, but she followed Kelly into the house, down the hall and through to the kitchen. When they reached the dining area, Kelly turned round and surveyed her with steely eyes. Chloe knew that expression. It was the one Daniel wore when he was a hair's breadth from losing his temper.

'Do you know…?' she asked, with a quiver in her voice, her pitch rising. 'Do you know what it took for him to ask you that—in front of all those people?'

She nodded dumbly.

'Then why, for God's sake, didn't you say yes?' Kelly shouted, then remembered the two sleeping boys upstairs and curtailed her volume.

'I…I…'

Kelly's eyes narrowed. 'Yeah, I got that much on the evening news last night.'

Chloe's head swam and she had to close her eyes to regain her balance. The evening news.

And Kelly had seen it?

'I'm so sorry,' she mumbled, and met Kelly's fiery gaze.

'And then you just left him to sit it out here, waiting for his plane, didn't even explain... Didn't even *talk* to him afterwards!'

'I couldn't!' Chloe replied. 'They—the PR team—they whisked us off in opposite directions. I tried to get to him, but everything was going wild... There were microphones and reporters everywhere.' She shook her head. 'Even if I could have got to him, he wouldn't have wanted it aired for the whole nation to see! I decided I would wait a bit...talk to him once the fuss died down...'

Kelly's expression softened a little. 'So why didn't you?'

'He wouldn't answer his phone. I thought maybe—' a small hiccuping sob caught her by surprise '—maybe he just needed some space...'

And then a big fat tear rolled down her cheek.

Kelly puffed out a breath. 'Sounds about right. You know Daniel... He doesn't do *crushed*, he does *angry* instead.'

Chloe nodded. 'That's what I thought. But I couldn't let him go without talking to him.' Oh, help. Here came the tears again, and this time they'd brought reinforcements.

Kelly pulled out a dining chair and motioned for Chloe to sit, then she did the same. 'Why did you say no?' she asked, her features drooping. 'You love him, don't you?'

Chloe hiccuped again and nodded vehemently. 'We've hardly even talked for weeks...'

'Because you asked him to leave you alone,' Kelly interjected, far too reasonably.

Oh, crap. She had, hadn't she?

'I wasn't sure...I'm still not sure...if he just said it as a knee-jerk thing, if that reporter kind of pushed him into it... If it's me he really wants,' she added, with a desperate look at Kelly, 'or if it's just the prize of getting me to say yes.' She swallowed. 'You know what he's like...'

'Yes, I do,' she said firmly. 'I know that he was broken inside until he met you, Chloe. I know he struggled to let himself care about anyone or anything.' Her expression grew grave. 'You've broken his heart, you know. He meant it. Every stupid word.'

Chloe felt a shiver start deep in her belly and work its way up through her body, through her shoulders and out of her mouth on a breath. 'I know,' she whispered. 'But meaning it and following through with it are two very different things. What if he changed his mind?' He had before. Twice. 'I couldn't live with it if he did it again,' she added, almost to herself.

Kelly shook her head. 'He's not like that,' she said, her eyes glistening a little. 'Believe me, if anyone knows about guys who run hot and cold, it's me. But Daniel... It takes him a bit of time to get there, but when he's in, he's all in.'

Something warm blossomed within Chloe, even as her stomach swirled with ice.

'Oh, Kelly... What have I done?' she whispered, and then louder, 'What time's his flight?'

Kelly was on her feet so fast her chair almost toppled backwards. 'He only left ten minutes before you knocked on the door. You could catch him with a fast enough driver.' But then she pressed her lips together and shook her head again. 'I don't know how you're going to get him to listen to you, though. The kind of foul mood he was in this morning won't lift for at least another week. The idiot will probably fly the plane himself to avoid talking to you at the moment.'

'Oh.' Chloe felt dizzy. There were too many things to think about. 'I don't have a car.'

'I do,' Kelly said, and then she ran to the bottom of the stairs and yelled, 'Boys! Get your coats and shoes on! We're going on an adventure.' Moments later a pair of dark heads appeared in the kitchen doorway.

'Cool!' Cal said, putting his wellington boots on the wrong feet. Ben didn't say anything—he was too busy watching his brother and copying everything he did. Including the wellies.

'Can we really get there in time?' Chloe asked breathlessly.

'I can outgun any cabby in London,' Kelly replied, 'but that still doesn't mean he's going to listen to you.'

For a moment her brain froze, too terrified by Kelly's words to think of any way round it, but then she said, 'I can think of one way to get his undivided attention for at least a couple of seconds. But I need to borrow some lipstick—the brightest and reddest you've got.'

Kelly looked her up and down. It was true that Chloe was not looking her best. She was wearing leggings with a ratty old pullover and her long red coat slung over the top. 'Honey,' Kelly said, 'you can borrow whatever you want. But I think you're going to need a hell of a lot more than lipstick.'

* * *

Daniel stared at Alan's back as they queued to go through airport security. He shuffled forward, passport in hand, handing it over when required and receiving it back without even noticing if it had been a man or a woman who'd inspected it. All he could think about was the journey ahead of him. Almost twenty-four hours on two planes. That was a long time to sit and think.

And, to be honest, the *sitting* part didn't worry him so much.

'Daniel!'

The shout came from behind him. Instantly, his skin puckered into goosebumps. He turned on autopilot, even as his brain was screaming at him to keep walking forward.

He wasn't ready for this.

Wasn't ready to talk to her, wasn't ready to see her.

But he was...seeing her. Just the other side of the passport check desks, behind a clump of queueing travellers. She wore a look of ragged desperation, her forehead bunched, her eyes pleading. Even with her hair a total uncombed mess she was still the most beautiful thing he'd ever seen. His rib muscles spasmed, squeezing his chest cavity.

He held her gaze for a second, then turned away.

He knew she was soft-hearted under all that gloss, that she wanted to explain—or, even worse, apologise— but he just wasn't ready.

He was one of those flies, caught in a pitcher, who'd worked it out and had given up struggling. Only one thing left to do now... Drown in that clear, sticky fluid while slowly being digested alive. None of that lovely drugging, narcotic syrup for him, though. He would feel every second of it. So, no, he couldn't look at her again. Not because he hated her, not because he didn't love her. Quite the reverse.

There was some kind of commotion going on behind him. He ignored it at first, but then he heard her again. 'Daniel Bradford, don't you dare run!'

He froze.

'I love you!' She yelled it so loud that everyone in the security queue stopped and he smacked into Alan's back.

'Flipping hell,' Alan said, turning round, his eyes going wide.

Daniel couldn't resist any longer. He spun round to find Chloe balanced on top of a trolley piled with cases, elevating her above the crowd. Where she'd hijacked it from, he had no idea.

Her gaze connected with his and locked. Not so much desperation in those eyes now as determination. Without looking away, she fumbled with the tie on her coat. Then she pulled both the edges wide, her chin tilted up.

Daniel's heart stopped. Now she had his full and undivided attention.

'Flipping hell,' Alan mumbled again.

There wasn't much under that coat. But not fancy knickers. Plain, functional underwear. Didn't matter to him. She was still spectacular. But it was the bit *between* bra and pants that really caught his attention. Scrawled there in bright red...something...were some words.

I do! it read above her belly button in large block capitals, and beneath, *Do you?*

All this happened in a matter of seconds. When she'd seen he'd read and understood, the coat closed again and she knotted the tie firmly round her waist. Just as well, really. Already he could see a couple of security guards looking her way, trying to work out what all the fuss was about.

With no more distractions, his gaze was drawn back to her face. He could see it all there now—the pain, the embarrassment of what she'd just done, the apology he wouldn't have listened to any other way and, most importantly, the truth. The love.

I do.

Do you...?

He looked over his shoulder at Alan, standing behind him open-mouthed, and then back to Chloe.

He *so* did.

And then he was shoving his way past the half dozen people who'd piled through the passport check after him. Alan reached out and grabbed his sleeve.

'Hey! Where are you going? You just can't—'

Daniel wrenched his arm free and looked his colleague in the face. 'There'll be another plane tomorrow,' he said, 'but there won't be another woman like this one. Not for me.'

The two of them stared at each other, then Alan shrugged. 'Fair enough.'

When he turned again the crowd had melted away. People were standing back and grinning expectantly, leaving a clear path between him and the woman in the red coat—off the trolley now—hands clasped together and a million questions in her eyes.

And, off to the side, with his nephews, was his sister. Yup. He should have guessed she'd had something to do with this.

But he didn't care about the whys and wherefores now; he just ran to Chloe, scooped her up so her feet left the floor and delivered the kiss he'd been holding back for far too long. From the response she gave him, he'd guess she had one of her own to let loose.

'I'm sorry...so sorry...' she mumbled between kisses.

He pulled back, caught her face between his palms and waited for her to open her eyes. Her lids fluttered open. She focused on him and swallowed.

'You took me by surprise,' she said softly, her eyes glistening. 'I *do* love you. I do want to be with you. It was just a lot to take in unexpectedly. I panicked...'

Daniel leaned in and kissed her, communicating his understanding the best way he knew how. Softly. Tenderly. Skin upon skin. After all, there had been more times when she'd been the brave one, had hung everything she felt on the line, and he'd been the one to back away.

There was a not-so-subtle cough beside him, disguising the phrase *Get a room!* in his sister's dulcet tones. He smiled against Chloe's lips then broke contact. Her eyes were closed and she looked blissfully happy, totally lost. Good. So was he.

But then her lids snapped open and she looked at the departures board, panic written all over her features. 'Oh, Daniel! Your plane...'

He shook his head. 'It can leave without me. Borneo can wait another twenty-four hours.'

She clung onto him, buried her face in his shoulder. 'I'm going to miss you so much.'

'Come with me,' he whispered into her ear.

She pulled away and stared at him. 'I can't! My job—'

He silenced her with a quick, hot kiss. 'I started badgering the powers that be about the sudden need for an orchid expert on the team. Seven hundred species on that mountain alone...'

Chloe shook her head, her eyes full of disbelief. 'You didn't!'

He grinned at her. 'I did. And they said yes. It was supposed to be a surprise. I was going to tell you last night, but things didn't exactly go according to plan.'

She blinked at him, as if she couldn't quite make sense of what he was saying.

'If you want, you can join us next week,' he added.

That was when Chloe launched herself at him and kissed him until he couldn't remember if he was here because he was supposed to be getting on a plane or whether he'd just come off one.

'Oh, for goodness' sake,' a grumpy-voiced Kelly said somewhere to his left. 'At this rate we're never going to make it out of the airport.'

'Up there!'

Chloe pushed the damp hair back out of her eyes and looked where Daniel was pointing. The sun filtered through the canopy above their heads in shafts, dappling the rainforest floor with gold, lighting up the backs of leaves and adding yet more shades of green into the endless forest.

'Where?' She couldn't see anything.

Daniel came in close behind her. Much closer than a colleague on a seed-collecting expedition should. Thankfully, he was much more than that. No ring as yet—no time to shop—but she didn't care about that.

And this, what he was giving her now, was so much more than metal and stones. That could come later.

She followed the line of his finger to a fallen log, its bark almost completely obscured by the ferns and mosses and creepers that clung to it.

'Oh!'

She saw it—the distinctive yellow and brown stripes of the rare slipper orchid. Her heart lurched. She wanted to go and see it up close, but first there was something she wanted to do even more. She turned towards him, sliding round under his outstretched arm, and pressed a kiss to his chin as she wound her arms around his neck.

'I was pretty clever proposing to you,' she said. 'Not many women get to marry a man who makes their long-cherished dreams come true.'

Daniel went still and stared down at her. There was a definite hint of challenge in his eyes. 'That's not quite right, is it?' he replied, slipping his arms under hers around her torso. '*I* proposed to you.'

She nodded, and one eyebrow lifted a little. 'Yes, you did, but—'

'I asked first,' he interjected. 'You wouldn't have pulled that stunt if it hadn't been for me.'

She licked her lips and looked sideways before returning her gaze to him. 'Yes,' she said, 'but mine's the one that stuck.'

He opened his mouth to argue, but she stalled him with a kiss. 'Shut up,' she said. 'We've got an orchid to catalogue.'

And after that, they had the rest of their lives to argue that one out.

* * * * *

COMING NEXT MONTH FROM

kiss™

Available March 19, 2013

#9 THE SECRET WEDDING DRESS by Ally Blake

Paige Danforth isn't interested in setting herself up for an *un*happy-ever-after—she knows the closest she'll ever get to walking down the aisle is as a bridesmaid. But one bridal sale later Paige is left clutching her dream wedding dress! Will commitment-phobic Gabe Hamilton stick around when he discovers not only skeletons...but a lavish white designer creation in her closet?

#10 DRIVING HER CRAZY by Amy Andrews

Journalist Sadie Bliss is on a mission to prove herself as a world-class reporter. But when she embarks on a road trip across the Australian Outback with dangerously mouthwatering photographer Kent Nelson, she suddenly longs to throw her rule book out the car window. After all, what happens in the Outback stays in the Outback...*right?*

#11 WHY RESIST A REBEL? by Leah Ashton

Ruby Bell has put scandal and relationships behind her to forge a successful career in film. Then the talk of Hollywood himself, actor Devlin Cooper, strolls onto her set after being fired from his past two movies. He's looking decidedly devilish, but the last thing she needs is Dev making outrageous demands...and proving that no one can resist a bad boy....

#12 HER MAN IN MANHATTAN by Trish Wylie

It seems mayor's daughter Miranda Kravitz has scored herself a *very* dreamy bodyguard! Apparently the fireworks between them are scorching, but will this tabloid darling *really* be willing to give up her newfound taste for freedom—no matter how gorgeous Tyler Brannigan is? And will Tyler be able to keep this Manhattan princess in check without resorting to the use of handcuffs...?

HKCNM0313

REQUEST YOUR FREE BOOKS!
2 FREE NOVELS PLUS 2 FREE GIFTS!

YES! Please send me 2 FREE Harlequin® Kiss novels and my 2 FREE gifts (gifts worth about $10). After receiving them, if I don't wish to receive any more books, I can return the shipping statement marked "cancel." If I don't cancel, I will receive 4 brand-new novels every month and be billed just $4.30 per book in the U.S. or $4.99 per book in Canada. That's a savings of at least 13% off the cover price! It's quite a bargain! Shipping and handling is just 50¢ per book in the U.S. and 75¢ per book in Canada.* I understand that accepting the 2 free books and gifts places me under no obligation to buy anything. I can always return a shipment and cancel at any time. Even if I never buy another book, the two free books and gifts are mine to keep forever.

145/345 HDN FVXQ

Name	(PLEASE PRINT)

Address	Apt. #

City	State/Prov.	Zip/Postal Code

Signature (if under 18, a parent or guardian must sign)

Mail to the **Harlequin® Reader Service:**
IN U.S.A.: P.O. Box 1867, Buffalo, NY 14240-1867
IN CANADA: P.O. Box 609, Fort Erie, Ontario L2A 5X3

Want to try two free books from another line?
Call 1-800-873-8635 or visit www.ReaderService.com.

Trish Wylie brings you a contemporary story
of love, rebellion and trust with

HER MAN IN MANHATTAN

"I'm in your life now. Get used to it."

The flecks of gold that flared in her eyes hinted at a temper
to match her hair. For a split second he wanted her to get mad
enough to swing for him—to spit fire and passion and remind
him of the woman he'd kissed.

As if sensing a weakness ripe for exploitation, she switched
tactics. The curve of her full lips became sinful, drawing his
gaze to her mouth and calling him to taste her again. She
slowly ran the tip of her tongue over the surface, leaving a
hypnotically glossy sheen in its wake.

In an instant he remembered how she'd felt when her body
was melded to his, how soft her skin had been beneath his
fingertips and how badly he'd burned for her. Just as suddenly
he was aware of how close they were standing. One more step
and their bodies would be touching again.

It took almost as much effort not to frown at his reaction as
it did to snap his gaze back up to her eyes. "That won't work
either, so you can forget it."

"I have no idea what you mean."

Sure she didn't. He reached for the door handle and jerked
his chin. "Back up a step."

The battle of wills made the air between them crackle, and
when her gaze briefly flickered to his mouth Tyler knew *that*

kiss was as much on her mind as it had been on his. Her awareness of him was in the darkening of her eyes, in the increased rise and fall of her breasts. Any hope he'd had that what had happened between them could be blamed on the heat of the moment was gone. But while he'd lost his self-control once, he wasn't about to let it happen again.

"You getting in or am I putting you there?"

"You can't manhandle me like a common criminal," she replied on a note of outrage.

"Try me."

She glared at him as she took a step back. *"Door."*

Tyler held it open, unable to resist an incline of his head and a sweep of his arm in invitation. "Your highness…"

**Find out what happens next in
HER MAN IN MANHATTAN by Trish Wylie,
on sale March 19, 2013,
wherever Harlequin books are sold.**

Use this coupon to
SAVE $1.00
on the purchase of
ANY 2
Harlequin KISS books.

Available wherever books are sold, including most
bookstores, supermarkets, drugstores and discount stores.

- ✂ - - -

SAVE $1.00 ON THE PURCHASE OF **ANY TWO** HARLEQUIN KISS BOOKS.

Coupon expires July 31, 2013. Redeemable at participating retail outlets
in the U.S. and Canada only. Limit one coupon per customer.

52610686

CANADIAN RETAILERS: Harlequin Enterprises Limited will pay the face
value of this coupon plus 10.25¢ if submitted by customer for this product
only. Any other use constitutes fraud. Coupon is nonassignable. Void if
taxed, prohibited or restricted by law. Consumer must pay any govern-
ment taxes. Void if copied. Nielsen Clearing House ("NCH") customers
submit coupons and proof of sales to Harlequin Enterprises Limited,
P.O. Box 3000, Saint John, NB E2L 4L3, Canada. Non-NCH retailer—for
reimbursement submit coupons and proof of sales directly to Harlequin
Enterprises Limited, Retail Marketing Department, 225 Duncan Mill Rd.,
Don Mills, ON M3B 3K9, Canada.

5 65373 00033 5   (8100)1 18300

U.S. RETAILERS:
Harlequin Enterprises Limited will
pay the face value of this coupon
plus 8¢ if submitted by customer
for this product only. Any other
use constitutes fraud. Coupon is
nonassignable. Void if taxed,
prohibited or restricted by law.
Consumer must pay any govern-
ment taxes. Void if copied. For reimbursement submit coupons and proof
of sales directly to Harlequin Enterprises Limited, P.O. Box 880478, El Paso,
TX 88588-0478, U.S.A. Cash value 1/100 cents.

HKCOUP0213A